THE WISHING WELL

Natalie Kleinman

SAPERE
BOOKS

THE WISHING WELL

Published by Sapere Books.

24 Trafalgar Road, Ilkley, LS29 8HH,
United Kingdom

saperebooks.com

ISBN: 978-1-80055-947-9

CHAPTER ONE

Kent, February 1818

Harriet Lambert stared unseeingly out of the window of her childhood home, unconsciously gripping the curtain whose green hue was almost an exact match for her eyes. Beyond the manicured lawn and ornamental gardens of Merivale House, situated just north of Faversham, lay the Kent marshes, as bleak as her mood and no less forgiving. She loved them nonetheless and would have much preferred, even in the cold, to be running barefoot in the wilderness than packing for a trip to London.

It had been three years since she'd last been to the capital, filled then with excitement and anticipation. During her first season she had met and become betrothed to the dashing John Downing, home on leave from the army and the epitome of any young girl's dream. And he had chosen her. He had been her most persistent admirer, casting all others aside in his determined pursuit, practically haunting the house in Hay Hill and leaving posies when he found her away from home. In the short time they had known each other they had fallen in love, and John had sought her father's permission to marry his daughter.

"Young cub was determined to have you, Harriet. There was no denying him. In any case, he's a nice chap. I like him," Papa had informed her, "so it's up to you now."

The young soldier had proposed to Harriet with all the romance she could have wished for. Splendid in his uniform, laughter in his eyes, down on one knee, he had been impossible to resist, nor had she wished to. But she had met him, loved him and lost him in the space of one short month. His furlough over, he had returned to his battalion and become another statistic in the war, losing his life at Waterloo and leaving Harriet totally bereft. For a while she had been inconsolable, but it all seemed so long ago now. These days she found it difficult even to remember what he looked like.

"Come, Harry, and help me if you will to write a letter of thanks to Aunt Matilda," her younger sister said, bursting into the room. "She has been most generous and has sent me an amount of money which I'm certain I shall never be able to spend."

Harriet dragged her eyes from the view and smiled at Amabel's naivety. "Don't think it, my darling. Before long it will be gone and you will be begging Mama for some pin money to purchase some furbelow or other which you absolutely cannot do without."

Amabel sat on Harriet's bed, eyes round with astonishment, for she had never seen such a large sum. "I was still in the schoolroom when you went to London. I was overcome with envy, I can tell you."

"And so you did, often and often."

Both laughed at the memory.

"So much has happened since then. Papa has passed on and you, poor thing, were mourning on two fronts. Do you do so still, Harry?" Amabel asked, her tone all at once more sober. "You looked so wistful when I came in."

"I admit you caught me in a weak moment, but they are fewer these days. I like to think that John was happy in those last weeks. But this is no time for reflection," she asserted, though that was indeed what she had been indulging in. "Like

Cinderella, you shall go to the ball. You shall go to many balls. And you will shine at every one."

Amabel jumped up once more and embraced her sister, her finger tweaking one of Harriet's chestnut curls. "As will you, my dearest. It is time for you to re-enter the world," she said, with a maturity that belied her eighteen years. Harriet feigned an enthusiasm she was far from feeling and they went off arm in arm to compose the letter to their aunt.

That afternoon the sisters were sitting with their mother, Louisa Lambert, in the drawing room. The soft pink furnishings added to the homeliness of the space, which was designed for comfort, rather than to impress. Each woman was engaged in a different task. Harriet was struggling to set some stitches in the fading light and leaned towards the inadequate glow from the candles on the small table beside her. Amabel was leafing through some fashion plates and Louisa was pouring tea.

"Are we to set off next Wednesday as planned, Mama?" asked Harriet. "There are still some tenants I must visit before we leave. You know how meticulous Papa always was about addressing his duties, and we shall be gone for many weeks."

Louisa looked up. "And like your father, you are not content to allow Mr Butterfield to fulfil those obligations on our behalf," she said with a smile.

Harriet was astonished that her mother should even consider such a thing, but in truth her interest in the estate and the attendant responsibilities that had fallen to her upon Percival Lambert's demise had contributed to her own salvation. It was her way of dealing with the grief of two tragedies, one coming so hard upon the other. She wasn't one to delude herself and realised that the youthful passion she had felt for John

Downing had softened over time into a fond but less painful memory. Her closeness to her father, and their shared love of riding which had led them to spend some part of almost every day together, made the loss of her parent harder to bear. It was that keenness for the outdoors that had caused her to pick up her father's reins. While Edward Butterfield was as good a steward as they could wish for, she held the same belief as Papa that a good leader made for a contented workforce.

"You know my feelings on that score, Mama."

"I do, and I am fairly certain that given the choice you would remain here at Merivale rather than come to London."

Harriet's eyes flickered hopefully for a moment, but she realised it was out of the question and quite unfair to both her mother and her sister.

Louisa was quick to notice and her heart went out to her daughter. "It won't do, you know." Sympathy was evident in her voice. "Aside from the fact that wild horses wouldn't drag Amabel to the city without you, it's time you found your own place in society. You cannot remain forever buried in Kent."

"I know it, Mama. You have been more than patient with me, and I do not want to be a burden to you."

"A burden! How can you even think it? But we must consider the future, you know. The estate is not encumbered, as you are aware, but it would break my heart for you to dwindle here into an old maid. You should have a family of your own."

Harriet went to her mother and hugged her affectionately, her ready smile breaking through and causing Louisa to relax once more. "No-one could become an old maid in any establishment in which you resided, Mama, with your love of life and joy in all things ridiculous. I am more likely to become a child once more, sitting on the floor with you playing jackstraws or climbing the trees in the orchard."

"I agree," said Amabel. "I don't believe I have ever beaten you at that game, Mama."

"No, only your father was more adept than I," said Louisa. A sharp look of pain could be seen in her features before she turned the subject to the forthcoming trip, answering Harriet's original question. "Yes, I have arranged to take occupation of the house in Hay Hill on Thursday, so we shall depart on Wednesday and stay overnight before arriving on that day. Better to take our time at this season than to risk not arriving until after dark."

"In that case, Amabel, you must study those plates assiduously, for if my own experience is anything to go by, Mama will drag you from shop to shop to ensure you are dressed in the highest fashion. How lucky you are with your blonde hair and blue eyes. There is hardly a colour suitable for a girl of your age that you will not be able to wear."

On Tuesday of the following week, Harriet was ensconced in the library with Butterfield, going over the accounts and finalising the small details.

"And be sure, if you will, to visit the Thompson family to enquire after Jack. His leg should be healed soon, but I would not wish you to be backwards with any attention," she said earnestly.

Butterfield smiled. "Of course, Miss Lambert, and I shall take with me some fruit from the hothouse. Was there anything else you wished me to attend to in your absence?"

Harriet laughed at him, knowing full well that he was teasing her. That was what happened when someone had known you from a child. "I have no doubt you have everything in hand,

Edward, but you need only write to me in Hay Hill if there is anything that causes you concern."

"Yes, and have you running straight back here to deal with it yourself."

Chuckling but not denying it, Harriet left him to visit the stables and to speak with the head groom, Ben Jones.

She spent some while in the stable block, checking on each horse in its stall. Both her mother and Amabel rode occasionally and each had their own mount. Then, aside from the carriage horses, there was Old Thunder who pulled the gig and Apollo, her father's horse. She'd been unable to part with him and it was Ben's job now to exercise him each day. Finally she came to Rhapsody, who was saddled and ready for her. This was to be their final ride together before Harriet's departure the next day.

With the sun glinting on her golden mane, Rhapsody's hooves clattered as they trotted out of the yard, her excitement as palpable as her rider's. The next hour passed in deep contentment for both. All too soon it was over and, as Harriet unsaddled the horse and removed Rhapsody's bridle, Ben leaned over the gate. He watched as she took up a brush and began to work on the mare's coat.

"I could do that for you if you like," he offered.

Harriet glanced up. "Is it likely I would let you, Ben? Already I am missing her, and I haven't even gone yet. This will be our longest ever parting for, as you well know, Papa bought her for me upon my return from London three years ago, after…"

She broke off, her emotions preventing her from continuing, but he knew exactly what she meant. Her father had purchased the pretty mare soon after they had learned of John Downing's death. His hope was that she might lose herself, for a short while at least, in her pleasure in the horse. And then he too had died, far too young, from an inflammation of the lungs. He had been right, though. For a long time, her only moments of solace had been while out with her favourite.

"Ben…?" she began.

"Don't you worry none, miss. I'm too heavy for her but Arthur will ride her every day, and she'll be waiting for you when you come home."

Harriet nodded her approval — she trusted Arthur Mason, the under groom, as much as Ben.

Having reassured her, Ben walked away, leaving her to enjoy her last moments with Rhapsody.

The next morning the ladies made an early start, the footman having only twice been bidden to return to the house for some forgotten item. Sam Coachman was to drive the carriage, followed by another which held their maids and was piled with as much luggage as Louisa deemed necessary for a visit to the capital. Harriet was happy enough to sit facing the rear, thus affording her sister a better opportunity to give her attention to countryside she had never before passed through. An early mist had given way to a cold but sunny day, and Amabel's excitement was infectious. She whiled away what might have been a tedious time with questions and observations.

They stopped at a very pretty inn for refreshment before continuing on to The Plough, where they were to spend the night. There they retired soon enough for, though the journey had been interesting, they were all ready for their beds and keen to start afresh the next day. Following an early breakfast, the party set off in good time and arrived in Hay Hill in the middle of the afternoon, no incident having occurred to disrupt their passage. Louisa had had the forethought to hire the same house they had stayed in during Harriet's first season, so there was nothing to give them a disgust of the place. Amabel dragged her sister from room to room, inspecting each one with great enthusiasm. Meanwhile, their mother sat in a comfortable chair in the morning room in front of a welcoming fire and, though she wouldn't have admitted it, fell into a comfortable doze.

Later that day, the women were making themselves comfortable in the parlour.

"Tomorrow we must pay a visit to your Aunt Matilda, Amabel, for I would not wish to be backward in observing any attention. I had not looked for such generosity from her, I must say," said Louisa.

"Nor I, Mama, and truthfully I am at a loss to understand it."

"That is because you cannot remember her visiting us at Merivale when you were still in leading reins. I am aware that you have seen her several times since, but at the time you bounced over to her and threw your chubby arms around her neck. I do believe that was the source of her affection for you. With no children of her own and you being her only brother's child, it is not surprising she takes an interest in you."

Harriet laughed. "She gave me no such distinction, and who shall blame her? I was a bit of a tomboy, even at five years old. I remember Papa telling me a long time after that I had behaved abominably, bringing in my dirt from the stables and interrupting her when she asked him a question. I don't believe I was a very engaging child."

Neither her mother nor her sister had any difficulty in attributing truth to this tale, Louisa going so far as to say, "You may have grown into a beautiful young woman, Harriet, but I don't consider you to have outgrown your hoydenish tendencies even now — you are just more in control of them these days. When you wish to be, that is."

"Ah, there's hope for me yet then," she replied, and left the room still chuckling.

CHAPTER TWO

Paris, February 1818

"I'm bored, Gil. I want to go home," said Major Brew Ware, throwing his cards on the table with a sigh.

"So early? The evening has hardly begun."

"No, home. To England."

Gil Carstairs could not have been more surprised had his friend declared the intention of taking holy orders.

"Are you mad? This is Paris, old boy! Why on earth would you want to leave?"

"For any number of reasons," Brew replied, his impatience showing in the way he ran his fingers through his longer than fashionable dark blond hair. It fell back onto his forehead, as untamed as its owner.

"What about the fashions? What about the women? Or should I say woman? Delphine?"

"Fashion is more your department than mine. My tastes are simple. Exacting but simple. As for Delphine, that little affair has run its course, I believe. For her as much as for me. And don't forget, you have only been in France for a short while, whereas I... The truth is, Gil, that I long to plant my feet once again on English soil."

"You would leave while you're on such a winning streak?"

"A card game is a card game, whether it be in Paris, London or Rome. And the money isn't important anymore."

"You didn't used to think that." Gil was as good-humoured as ever and, being well-heeled in his own right, he was in no way envious of the vast fortune his companion had accumulated from his gift as a player.

The wealth Brew had so wished for as a boy meant little to him now. He remembered a day, long ago, when he had stood at the well behind his home, a home he hadn't seen for several years now. He squeezed his eyes tight shut, now as then, but this time by reason of an ache for something lost. The war in which he had been so eager to take part had been over for nearly three years, but he still considered his time in the army as the happiest of his life. He had no regrets about running away from England to enlist, and it hadn't been long before he had distinguished himself in battle and his bravery had been recognised. By the time the hostilities had come to an end, he had attained his majority and friendships had been forged which he knew would hold for life. After that he had remained in France, certain that the rift with his father was too wide to mend. A talent for gaming had left him well able now to purchase the commission he had once so desired, but he had no ambition to be part of an army in peacetime. Brew was a man without direction, and it didn't sit well with him.

He became aware that Gil was speaking once more.

"Will you go to London or Austerly?"

Brew smiled and his face was transformed to that which had drawn men to him so often in the past. And women too. "You think my father would welcome me home with open arms?"

His words drew no answering smile from Gil. "I think it time you healed the rift between you."

"It was not of my making."

"Are you so sure of that?"

The humour vanished as Brew's face became twisted. Staring at his friend across the table, he leaned forward onto his elbows and said, "You will admit he must take some of the responsibility."

"You didn't make it easy for him."

"He didn't understand."

Gil had been Brew's ally since childhood, their homes in Lincolnshire lying adjacent to each other. He knew, perhaps more than any other, how deep had been the craving for action.

"No more than you understood him. Or sympathised. Do you really believe him to have been unaware of your ambition? How painful do you think it was that he couldn't furnish you with the only thing you ever really wanted? And after what happened, he needed you at Austerly and you abandoned him."

Gil spoke not critically but with the privilege of familiarity and the deep affection each held for the other. Brew would not expect softly worded phrases to cushion the blow, and his friend would be nothing less than honest. He had not written home and, had it not been for Gil's correspondence with his own family, for all Brew's parents knew he might well have been dead. Napoleon was tucked away safely on St Helena, but something had prevented young Ware from putting pen to paper. The longer it went on, the harder it had become.

"There's still time, you know," Gil continued quietly. "To repair the damage."

Brew randomly picked up one of the cards that were scattered on the table and turned it face up. The Ace of Diamonds. He smiled again, this time with genuine amusement. "Well, if this is anything to go by, the attempt ought to be crowned with success."

"Are you serious? Will you try?"

"It's been so long, Gil. It may be too late."

"But you'll try?"

"I don't know. I'll consider it."

Two days later, the men set off for England. Austerly was not Brew's immediate destination on reaching the country of his birth. He and Gil headed first for London.

"I'm astonished you have come with me, my friend," said Brew. "I had thought the lightskirt you had in your keeping in Paris might have persuaded you to remain."

"The truth, Brew, is that like you I was becoming bored. I wasn't ungenerous. She certainly seemed quite satisfied with the necklace I gave her as a parting gift."

"I'm sure your open-handedness was only exceeded by your charm. Do you have plans to return to Langborne?"

"Not immediately. I must pay an urgent visit to my tailor. I have become tired of French fashion and need a change. I'm of the opinion that this will be a period of change for both of us, don't you think?"

Brew looked around the large room in the hotel where they were lodging until he could find a house he liked sufficiently to lease. It was opulent enough, and he smiled to think how far he had come since his modest beginnings. Moving across the room to pour a drink, he stumbled. Only his stick prevented him from taking a fall, a constant reminder of the legacy of his action during the war. Gil made no attempt to help him, knowing full well his intervention would not have been welcome.

The walking aid wasn't the only thing that set Brew apart from other men. He stood well above average height and, though his taste in clothes was less flamboyant than his friend's, Gil had to admit he cut an elegant figure and that black and silver formed a fine contrast to that unruly blond hair. Brew glanced back at the table, frustration showing in those piercing blue eyes — eyes that softened frequently, despite his attempts to distance himself from the world. They softened now as they rested on his friend before turning bleak as his thoughts ran elsewhere.

His sister, Becca, would be a young lady by now. How had she fared during the intervening years since last they'd met, he wondered? He felt guilty about having left her, when she'd been barely thirteen, at the mercy of their parents' grief as well as her own. By the time he'd left Austerly, eight years had passed since the terrible day that had changed all their lives forever, but the pain had been as raw as when the accident had happened. It was still.

"Sit down, man, and describe to me, if you would, the kind of residence you're looking for," Gil said in an attempt to distract him.

"As you well know, I am a stranger to London. I came here only once before leaving for France. I rely on you to tell me the best addresses, somewhere I can be in the hub of things."

"I thought you wanted to maintain a low profile?"

"And so I did, but I have changed my mind. You said it yourself. It is time to alter my way of life. I would, for instance, like to play cards for pleasure, not for gain. And, while I have no desire to be leg-shackled, I am nonetheless partial to the company of the fairer sex. It's true I have no title other than that of major, nor the expectation of one, but I am adequately well-born to make me acceptable in those circles I would wish to enter."

Gil raised one eyebrow and Brew laughed.

"You needn't look at me like that. I don't wish to take a mistress into my keeping. Not at the moment, anyway.

Delphine was … how shall I put it? Demanding. I'm looking for something simpler."

"When was anything in your life simple, my friend?"

"Never, and that's why I want to take advantage of your knowledge and establish some changes."

"Well, if you want my advice, you'll begin by engaging an agent to find a suitable property for you. You have only to tell him what you've just told me, and he will take upon himself all the difficulty of the task and hopefully leave you with nothing to do. In the meantime, we are comfortable enough here for some while to come if necessary."

Gil might well have stayed at the Carstairs family residence, but Brew had asked that he join him at the hotel and for the sake of present convenience he'd agreed to this arrangement. There would be sufficient time to move on when his friend was settled.

Over the next few days, Brew viewed only three houses and had no hesitation in opting for the third. It was situated in Grosvenor Square, and Brew was assured by both Gil and the agent that it was a good address.

"My own house is in Brook Street, just a few steps away, so I shall move back there now that you have a place of your own," said Gil.

It came already furnished and, although Brew knew he would have to make some changes — a painting in the library was sufficiently ugly to give him nightmares and was removed immediately — most could wait a while.

Gil had not had the same passion for the army that had consumed his friend since childhood. He had spent the war years in London, though he had been in France for much of the past twelve months of the ensuing peacetime. Home again, he began to visit his old haunts, taking Brew with him and introducing him to such places as commonly entertained men of fashion and substance. High on the list was a visit to the tailor, Weston, where both men spent a great deal of money. Whereas Gil's clothes were designed to draw attention to himself, for he delighted in causing a stir, Brew chose only his habitual black and silver. Both, though, were a gift to Weston, who was more than happy to dress two men of such stature. It was a pity, he thought, that Major Ware was afflicted with a limp, for he had a fine pair of calves and magnificent shoulders. However, his elegant figure set off his raiment to as great an advantage as its creator could have hoped for.

London was filling up rapidly as people returned for the start of the season, and it wasn't long before invitations were extended to both Brew and Gil, the one quiet and unassuming and the other full of open affability, but each with easy address and considered to be an asset to any party. All the time, though, at the back of Brew's mind was his promise to Gil that he would contact his father. This came rushing to the forefront when Gil's mother and father arrived in town, putting a bit of a damper on that young man's sense of freedom and causing him to suggest to Brew that he might move to his club for a while.

"Nonsense, man. There is ample room here in Grosvenor Square, should you wish. But what is this? I thought you and your parents rubbed along pretty well together."

Gil laughed and assured him it was so. "Only Mama persists in telling me it's time I settled down and started my own nursery. Now she's talking about introducing me to this or that young lady as a suitable bride. It is beyond bearing, Brew. I love her dearly, but her less than veiled comments are driving me to distraction."

"Well, you're more than welcome to stay with me. I just hope François and Gilbert don't come to blows," he said with a laugh. The rivalry between their valets was a source of amusement to both, for between those two worthies a rigid but jealous politeness was habitually sustained. "But if François leaves me, I shall hold you accountable."

Brew had always maintained an easy relationship with the Carstairs family, frequently haunting their home in Lincolnshire as a means of escaping his own. He wasted no time in paying them a visit and they welcomed him with enthusiasm. Sarah Carstairs, Gil's mother, could not help but notice the little lines about his eyes. Not having seen him for several years, she wondered if they were attributable to his time in the army or the greater tragedy that had befallen him at a much earlier age.

"Well, my boy, and how do you do?" asked her spouse, Matthew Carstairs. "I must say we are delighted to find you back in England. Funny lot, the French, or so I thought back in the days of my Grand Tour."

"I daresay things have changed somewhat since you were there, sir, but I am happy to be back on English soil."

"And do you plan to visit Austerly?" Matthew asked, to the dismay of his wife. He had always been a man to speak his mind, but she worried that this was a step too far under the circumstances. Indeed she could see that Brew visibly stiffened, but he replied with no edge to his voice.

"That will depend. I mean to write home to pay my respects."

"Good man. I make no doubt they will be happy to hear from you."

"Yes, sir," Brew said, feeling more like a small boy than a man of the world who had fought in the war. The conversation did, however, prompt him to take action. Upon his return home, he went straight to his library to draft a letter:

Father, I write to inform you that I am returned to England and am presently residing in Grosvenor Square.

He paused, having absolutely no idea how to continue. He rested his chin on his hand and stared unseeingly out of the window. The vision that haunted his dreams came to him once more. It made little difference if it were night or day. It rarely left him for more than a short while. He took up the pen once more.

I trust you and Mama are well and that my sister is happy. You must know that I enlisted in the army, though I was lucky enough to achieve the rank of major. I then remained in France at the end of the hostilities, but recently I have had the urge to come home.

Brew then decided that beating around the bush would serve no purpose.

It seems we have forever been estranged, though I know it is fifteen years since the awful day that changed all our lives. I said some things to you that were unforgivable, and you to me. Grief does strange things to a person, and we lived under the same roof for a further eight years with barely another word passing between us. Nothing will bring Nancy back, and in hindsight I take my share of the blame for what happened to her. I should not have left Austerly without a word to you or Mama of my intentions, and most assuredly I ought not to have left it so long to write. If you can find it in yourself to communicate with me, I can be reached at the address at the top of this page. Please give my fondest love to my mother.
Yours respectfully, Benedict Richmond Edward Ware (Brew)

He sat back in his chair, aware that he had broken out in a sweat. He read his letter through only once and sealed it before he could change his mind. Then he rang for his footman and asked that it be despatched immediately. After that he tried to put it out of his mind, but the question kept coming back to him. Would his father reply?

CHAPTER THREE

Harriet was trying hard to feel enthusiastic. While she was determined to support her sister, she had no desire to be presented to any eligible men. She couldn't help but acknowledge a certain justification in her mother's remarks about her future, but she also resented society's perception that the only suitable occupation for a woman of her class and upbringing was that of wife and mother. She knew she would be happy remaining at Merivale, but she knew equally well that Mama would not be so. The least she could do, for she loved her very dearly, was comply with her wishes by going with her and Amabel to London. That her mother was as hopeful for her as for her sister, Harriet had no doubt. It wasn't that she was averse to marriage, but she wanted romance, not a business arrangement. Having loved with all the intensity of youth, she had no expectation of ever experiencing such a degree of emotion again. However, she did want what her parents had had, for there could be no doubt that theirs had been a truly happy union.

It was difficult to argue with Louisa Lambert. A recognised beauty in her youth, she had married Percy in the face of parental opposition. They'd had aspirations of a title for her, but with a spirit her daughters had inherited from her, Louisa had rebelled and maintained that she would marry him and no other. For one of her generation this was unusually headstrong, but she'd had her way and never for a moment had she regretted it. And the fact that her husband was possessed of a large fortune went a long way to making the alliance more palatable to her parents.

Louisa was still a very attractive and gregarious woman. Her eldest daughter's chestnut hair and green eyes were a mirror for her own, but while Harriet was content to find fulfilment in running the estate, Louisa enjoyed nothing more than the company of others. She bore her widowhood with fortitude. The loss of her husband had been all the more painful because it had been unexpected, but after putting off her black she had been determined to take her place in the world once more. Independence was something else Harriet had inherited from her. It didn't always make for ease of companionship, but the respect they held for each other was unquestionable.

The visit to Aunt Matilda — or Lady Sawcroft, as she was known to society — had been received graciously, and Harriet was at pains to make a good impression, if only for Amabel's sake. She had received a rap on the knuckles from her aunt's fan together with the assertion that it was nice to see she had developed such pretty manners. "It is good to see that you have put that sad business behind you, and not before time," Matilda went on. "You will do very well, my dear. I have no doubt your mother will turn you both off in style."

A warning glance from Louisa prevented Harriet from responding honestly, and she said demurely that she hoped not to disappoint. The Lamberts spent more than half an hour with Lady Sawcroft, who was moved to state that Amabel's coming out ball should be held at St James's Square. Louisa thanked her sister-in-law and said that her younger daughter's introduction into society would begin slowly, with some small parties, so that Amabel might become accustomed to a way of life she had never before experienced. "Thereafter a ball in her honour will take place at Hay Hill," Louisa concluded.

Matilda bristled. "But what better place to fire her off than from her aunt's house?" she asked.

Louisa, who had expected something of the sort, had never in all her years of marriage allowed her sister-in-law to bully her, and she wasn't about to do so now. "Her mother's, of course. I thank you, we all thank you, for your generous offer, but I'm sure Amabel will be more comfortable in her own home."

"A hired house!"

"A very nice hired house. It served well enough for Harriet three years ago and will do the same for Amabel. No, don't take offence, Matilda. My mind is made up on this. Come, let us not quarrel. Instead let me thank you for your kind offer to hold a soirée here, which will cause you far less bother. That would be very welcome, and I would be most happy for her first foray into society to be under your aegis."

Matilda backed down, happy with the compliment and the compromise. She was so pleased with her nieces that as they left, she pressed largesse upon each of them, leaving them both astonished. In their carriage once more, Harriet looked at her mother with respect.

"You are a force to be reckoned with, Mama. No doubt Aunt Matilda thought to ride roughshod over you."

"I don't know how you had the courage to stand up to her. Kind as she has been to me, I am in awe of her whenever we meet," Amabel added.

"She should have known better. Neither your father nor I have ever given in lightly to her whims. She has a good heart, though, and I have a certain fondness for her."

Harriet looked at the money which she still held in her hand. "I didn't know how to accept her gift. I was never more surprised."

"She obviously considers you now to be a well-behaved and compliant young lady. If only she knew!"

All three were still laughing when they arrived back at Hay Hill.

Lady Sawcroft was as good as her word, and a card arrived inviting the Lambert ladies to attend a soirée in St James's Square seven days hence. Louisa considered the timing excellent, as it gave her more than sufficient time to kit out her daughters in a suitable manner. Nothing could be more detrimental to them than appearing as dowdy country cousins. Not that she was unduly modest about the appearance of either of her daughters. Both were of average height, but there the similarity between them ended. Harriet, with her stunning colouring, would always show to advantage almost regardless of what she might be wearing. Also, since she was not in her first season, she carried with her an assurance that only added to her appeal.

Amabel had all the advantages of a young woman blossoming from girlhood into a modest lady. Though she might naturally feel a certain degree of nerves, she would conduct herself well in company. She was all that a proud mother could wish, from her golden curls and her sparkling blue eyes all the way down to her dainty feet. Feet that had mastered every dance shown to her so that she moved effortlessly across the floor, able to hold a conversation without faltering. No, Louisa had no apprehension on behalf of either of her daughters. She looked forward to the future with the expectation of having a most enjoyable time.

"You look to be in good spirits, Harry," said Amabel, bouncing into the drawing room where Harriet was smiling at some recollection of her previous visit to London. "What has promoted such pleasure?"

Not wanting to depress her sister's spirits by admitting her thoughts had been of John Downing, she merely said, "I was wondering which emporium Mama proposes to take us to today. The choices seem to be endless, as does her energy." Her wry expression drove the smile from her face.

"Are you not enjoying yourself, Harry?" Amabel asked, eager for her sister to join in her delight.

Harriet suffered a moment of conscience, inwardly rebuking herself for not displaying more enthusiasm. "Of course I am! When have you ever known me to show a reluctance for shopping? Mama is determined to fit you out in the first style of elegance, and she has excellent taste. And when she has such a subject as you, the outcome can only be a happy one."

Amabel was a modest girl who considered her own blonde curls to be insipid. She would rather have inherited her mother's colouring, as her sister had done, and said so.

"Nonsense. You have a loveliness that will draw all to you. Just tell me before we depart, if you will, what colour ribbon I should choose for my straw bonnet. Ah, here is our mother now. Dearest Mama, I have only to fetch my pelisse and hat and I shall be ready. And, perhaps, Amabel, you might tell our parent of my quandary," Harriet said over her shoulder as she left the drawing room. "But not orange. No, with my colouring definitely not orange."

The shopping expedition was enjoyed by all three Lambert ladies. In addition to commissioning a number of gowns, various other items were purchased which Louisa told Harriet and Amabel would be indispensable to them in the coming weeks. Bonnets were chosen for both young ladies and another for their mother. Wherever they went, they were accommodated. Discounts were negotiated by Louisa and accepted by those shrewd purveyors of fashion in the knowledge that the Lambert ladies would display their wares to perfection, and no doubt enquiries would be made as to where they had purchased this hat or that gown.

When the day arrived for Matilda's soirée, Louisa accompanied her daughters to St James's Square at the allotted time. Harriet was dressed in a gown of deceptively simple cut, the cream cotton material gathered beneath the bodice. A design of roses and pale green leaves circled the hem and was repeated around the neckline and short puff sleeves, which lifted the dress above the ordinary. Slippers and a reticule of matching green silk completed the ensemble. Her sister, a vision in white with little rosebuds adorning her dress and two or three placed in her curls, looked everything a young woman ought to on her first society outing. Aunt Matilda greeted them with approval and said quietly to her sister-in-law, "You have done well, Louisa. I will give you this, you have excellent taste."

Aunt Matilda had assembled some thirty people for the evening, the cream of London society, for few would turn down an invitation from Lady Sawcroft. Harriet was delighted to renew her acquaintance with Julia Grantham, now married and with a babe at home. Both had come out in the same season and a friendship had formed between them. She had been the recipient of Harriet's confidences during her courtship and the shoulder on which she had shed her tears when news of John's demise reached London. It wasn't long before they put their heads together, conversing with the ease of long-standing acquaintances, even though it had been years since they had last met.

Harriet glanced up as two men approached, and she recognised one whom she had met once or twice when she was previously in town. She hadn't seen him since and was grateful that he remembered her.

"Miss Lambert, is it not?" he began. "How very nice to see you again. Allow me to introduce my friend, Major Ware, who is not long returned from abroad."

For a moment Harriet struggled to remember the young man's name, and it was obvious he was aware of it.

"Gil Carstairs," he supplied. "You may not recall. As I remember, your attention was elsewhere when last we met."

She could not construe his words as criticism for he was smiling kindly, evidently remembering how wrapped up she and John had been in each other, with eyes for no-one else. She smiled back appreciatively. "You must forgive my wretched memory, Mr Carstairs. It is a pleasure to see you again. And to meet you, Major," she added, turning to his friend. She introduced them in turn to Julia and to her mother and sister, who were sitting beside her. She then had leisure to observe both men as Major Ware addressed them all, but with his attention wholly focused on Amabel. She could not blame him. Her sister, in her opinion, outshone every other girl in the room. In contrast to the flamboyant apparel of his friend, Major Ware was dressed from head to toe in black and silver, his appearance so striking as to cause her to catch her breath.

"You will excuse me," he was saying, smiling warmly at her sister but addressing them all. "I am unable to request the pleasure of leading any of you ladies to the floor, but perhaps I may be permitted instead to procure some refreshment for you."

"If you please, sir, a glass of something cool would be very welcome to us all, I believe," Amabel answered.

He turned away to fulfil his errand, and it was only then that Harriet saw the walking stick that had previously been hidden from her view. That would explain his comment about not dancing. She wondered how he had sustained his injury. Another casualty of the wretched war? Her thoughts turned once again to John.

Gil, having been informed by Julia that her husband was in another room playing cards, invited her to dance with him and was absent when Major Ware returned, followed by a waiter carrying a tray of drinks. When everyone had been served, he took Julia's vacant chair and turned to speak to Harriet.

"I must rely on your indulgence if I may, Miss Lambert. I am a stranger to London and have very few acquaintances here. Gil has taken me under his wing and is determined that I shall mingle with society, but the truth is that at such a gathering as this one I am at a loss to remember the names of those to whom I have been introduced."

Was he alluding to her conversation with Gil? She raised a cool eyebrow and he laughed aloud, realising at once what her interpretation must have been. It transformed him, she thought, from a polite gentleman into one whom she might like to know better, something very rare for her these days.

"No, no, you misunderstand. I meant no disrespect. Indeed, I am grateful to speak with someone whose name I can remember." And then he seemed to realise that this comment too might be misconstrued. "I have once more put my foot in it, have I not? May I begin again? Miss Lambert, I am delighted to make your acquaintance. I am new to these parts and I'm looking for a friend."

Good heavens, the man was truly disarming.

"I'm sure you will have no difficulty in achieving your goal," Harriet replied.

"Is that a put down? Are you suggesting I look elsewhere?"

She laughed, drawn to this man as she had been to no other since John. "That would be cruel of me indeed." She turned the subject. "Mr Carstairs introduced you as Major Ware, but I believe I would have had no hesitation in putting you down as a military man. Somehow you all seem to carry yourselves differently."

"You speak as if you have some experience. Are you acquainted with many such?"

She felt her face fall, and she could tell that Major Ware was wondering what he might have said to distress her so much. "Forgive me. I was betrothed to John Downing and was introduced to several of his friends." A sigh escaped her lips. "Sadly he was killed at Waterloo."

"John Downing! Would you believe it, he was in my regiment. And a braver soldier you couldn't hope to meet. You must be very proud of him."

"I am. And of all the men who fought for our country. But I see you yourself didn't come away unscathed, Major Ware."

"There were many who came off far worse than I and, as you are only too aware, many who did not come home at all."

Harriet remembered something Gil Carstairs had said, and her curiosity prompted her to ask, "Your friend said you had not long returned to England, but the war has been over for three years now. Surely you haven't been in hospital all that time?"

Major Ware laughed, assuring her it had not been the case and saying that it was a much longer tale than he could tell her in one evening. Julia and Mr Carstairs returned and the major gave up his seat, saying that he hoped to have an opportunity to enlighten her in the near future.

CHAPTER FOUR

Gil declared his intention of paying a visit to the Lambert ladies the next morning, and Brew allowed himself to be persuaded to join him. He had enjoyed his conversation with the elder Miss Lambert and had been impressed by her self-assurance and direct approach. He wondered, however, whether she was still in mourning for John Downing, three years after his death. A pity if that were so.

The gentlemen were lucky to find the sisters at home. They were not so lucky to discover that several young bucks had had the same idea. Two of them were paying court to Amabel, vying for her attention in a way that her mama seemed to look upon with some amusement. As the newcomers were announced and made their bows, Gil, a man of much more address than the two youthful cubs before him, managed somehow to engage Amabel in conversation, at the same time dismissing the other gentlemen in the kindest possible way. Major Ware had to stop himself from laughing aloud when he received a desperate look from Harriet over the shoulder of the court card who was, he later learned, as boring a person as she had ever met.

"But surely his attire must have dazzled you, Miss Lambert," Brew said after the gentleman had retired and, as invited, he sat beside her. "If only he had removed his outer garment so we might have seen his waistcoat in all its splendour."

"Yes," she said with a chuckle, "I would indeed have been dazzled. In fact, I make no doubt I would have had to lie on my bed in a darkened room to cure me of the headache. Gold and luminous green stripes! Did you ever see such a thing?"

"I fear he was trying to emulate those members of the Four Horse Club, though the colours were wrong. In any case, your mother's drawing room is most assuredly not the place for such a display."

"And do you belong to that fraternity, Major?"

He smiled at her. Miss Lambert's question was said with an air of innocence, but there was something in her expression that told him she was teasing.

"I do not aspire to such heights nor, I think, could I bring myself to wear the mandatory blue waistcoat with yellow stripes. No, definitely not my style."

"Does your injury prevent you from handling the reins?"

Brew was taken aback for a moment. Miss Lambert came straight to the point in the same way she had the previous evening. "Not at all. I may not be a member of the esteemed club we have been discussing, but I believe I'm considered to have an aptitude. Perhaps I might prove it to you. Would you allow me to drive you in the park?"

Again she gave the delightful chuckle. "And now what must I say? I have put you in an untenable position. You are honour-bound, are you not, to offer to take me up?"

"You forget I have been in the army and am used to engaging in manoeuvres. I was under no such obligation and it would give me great pleasure. Now you must say, 'Yes please, Major Ware. I should be delighted.'"

"Yes please, Major Ware. I should be delighted."

"Tomorrow then, if you're free. Would you like me to ask your sister and Mr Carstairs to join us?"

She paused, apparently considering his proposal. "That sounds delightful," she replied after a moment.

Brew turned towards Gil, who was still speaking animatedly to the younger sister. "Gil, Miss Lambert has done me the honour of agreeing to drive out with me tomorrow, and we are hoping you and Miss Amabel might join us."

Amabel clasped her hands together, evidently delighted at the prospect. "May I, Mama?" she asked, turning excitedly to her mother.

"Of course you may. The weather looks set fair. You need only to ensure that you are dressed warmly enough."

A time was arranged and the two friends departed, the thoughts of each on the young lady he had just left.

"Would you care to stroll along to Jackson's?" Gil asked as they walked from Hay Hill. "It isn't too far from here."

Brew laughed. "I suspect my footwork wouldn't be up to dancing around a boxing ring."

"Damn it, man, I'm so sorry. I completely forgot. I don't notice any more, you see."

"No better a thing could you have said to me. I confess it doesn't trouble me as much as it used to. Perhaps the doctor was right after all."

"The doctor? What did he say?"

"Only that if I don't coddle myself it might improve with time. Though never," he added with a grin, "to the extent that I would take on anyone with even the smallest degree of pugilistic proficiency."

"But that's wonderful news. Perhaps a round or two would be good for you?"

"A little ambitious at this stage, I fear, but I'm happy to come and watch you."

"No, let us go instead to White's. It's even closer and requires far less energy." Gil linked arms with his friend and they turned about and headed in the direction of St James's Street. "Any word from Austerly yet?"

Brew missed a step. "No. It would seem my efforts towards a reconciliation were in vain."

"It's early days yet. Give him time."

Brew didn't believe it would make any difference. He still remembered how stern and unapproachable his father had become in his grief.

As they entered White's, they were greeted by a number of acquaintances and were solicited to play cards, an invitation which Gil declined but Brew accepted. It was something which still gave him much pleasure and, now that he no longer needed to earn his living this way, he was far more able to enjoy a game with friends. And he was gratified to find that he was making friends more easily than he had anticipated. Gil had shown him the way, but it was his own personality that attracted people to him. A quiet but dignified man, Brew spoke with a lot of good sense and was fast becoming a favourite on his own account. He spent the rest of the day at White's, leaving Gil to dine there while he returned to Grosvenor Square to spend a quiet evening at home.

Brew looked, as he did every time he returned to the house, to see what post might be laying on the ormolu table in the entrance hall. There was a bill from his tailor and one or two other sundry items but still no word from his father. Brew asked for a light supper to be sent to him in the library, where he settled down to read. He was still there when Gil returned at an advanced hour, clearly a little bosky. Nevertheless, they called for another bottle and spent a while in comfortable silence, with one or the other occasionally making some inconsequential comment.

"Did you ever see such beautiful blue eyes?" Gil asked all at once.

Brew had no trouble recognising to whom he referred. He smiled and said, "I'm glad I purchased that carriage as well as my curricle. I can see it will be very useful."

And so the two passed the rest of the evening in quiet companionship before retiring, both looking forward to tomorrow's drive.

Sadly the weather the next day proved to be surprisingly inclement and Brew received a note from the ladies, full of regret but saying they feared the treat must be postponed. He scribbled a hasty reply suggesting that he and Mr Carstairs might instead pay a visit to Hay Hill, where they could perhaps arrange the outing for a later date. He walked into the hall to hand it to the footman and found a silver tray being held out to him, on which lay a single letter.

"This has just arrived, sir. Would you like me to wait and see if there's to be a reply?"

Brew glanced down at it and his stomach sank to his knees. Even after all these years, he recognised his mother's writing. "No thank you, Grey. I'll read it at my leisure."

He crossed to the library, irritated to find his hands were shaking as he sat down and spread the sheet open before him on the table. He began to read:

My dearest boy

I have only today had sight of the letter you sent to your father some weeks ago. I had no idea you had written and can only say how happy I am to hear from you after all this time, though happy is not a strong enough word to convey my joy. I have missed you.

You will have realised by now that Papa is not intending to respond, but the very fact that he has shown the message to me after such a prolonged period (and not screwed it up and consigned it to the fire) speaks volumes, as it has obviously been preying on his mind. I can see no clear way of bringing about a rapprochement between you if he cannot acknowledge your extension of the olive branch. I fear he lost two children on that dreadful day.

I know I should not discuss your father's affairs but you are entitled to know, as his heir, that he struggles still with the estate and you will have no fortune to inherit upon his passing. However, it is fortuitous indeed that your letter came into my hand when it did, because I have some news which I hope will give you pleasure. Though we would never have been able to afford to launch your sister into society in a formal way, Rebecca has been fortunate indeed to have received a bequest from her godmother for whom she was named. I suspect she must have known something of our circumstances, for she stipulated that the money be spent exclusively on Becca's come out and I'm delighted to say there are sufficient funds for us to bring her to London for the remainder of the season. We are to arrive next week.

So, my darling boy, I beg that you will agree to see us during our stay. Your sister, I know, misses her big brother and I, well, there is no way to express my feelings. I grieve for Nancy every single day. Please let it be that I no longer have also to grieve for you.

Mama

Brew pushed his chair back from the table and, running his hand through his ever unruly hair, limped back and forth across the room. His heart was beating fast. His mother wanted to see him, though his father didn't. They would be here in a week, after all these years. An unaccustomed fear gripped him and he considered leaving London, but only for a moment. He had already waited far too long. By the time Gil burst into the room a few minutes later, he had himself under control. He decided, for the time being at least, not to mention the letter.

"This damnable weather, Brew! And I was so looking forward to seeing the Lambert sisters again."

"You are right, Gil, they have cried off, but I sent a note saying we would call later, so with any luck we will not be disappointed. Lovesick already, are you? And it's barely two months since you left your last sweetheart behind." But the smile left his face as his friend rounded on him.

"You will not speak of Miss Lambert in the same breath as Marianne, if you please."

He was evidently much distressed and Brew made his apologies immediately, assuring him he had meant no offence.

Gil laughed gruffly. "I can't believe it, Brew. This has never happened to me before. And she's only just come out. She has had no time to experience society. I cannot take advantage of her innocence, even were I to have the opportunity of doing so. I must be content to worship at her feet."

Gil, like many young men of a similar cut, was either *aux anges* or in deep despair. Brew, far more level-headed, reassured him that all was not lost and managed to coax him out of the sullens before they departed for Hay Hill later that day.

At least, Brew thought, *this has helped me put my own problems to the back of my mind for the time being.* He knew they would return later, but meanwhile he hoped to spend some time in the company of Miss Harriet Lambert, a young woman who, if he was any judge, had a reprehensible sense of humour.

Unsurprisingly, the drawing room at Hay Hill was somewhat crowded, the number of visitors being even greater than the last time they had called. It seemed the rain wasn't deterring young men from paying their respects to Mrs Lambert and her daughters. Even the court card in the striped waistcoat was there once again.

"You couldn't miss him in all that finery," Harriet remarked to Brew when he had managed to secure a seat beside her.

"You have no taste for such magnificence, Miss Lambert?"

"That is not how I should have described him. Look at your friend, Mr Carstairs, for example. While his attire is wont to make a statement, he doesn't deck himself out as to appear ridiculous. For myself, I prefer a more subdued style, but at least he looks to be a man of elegance and not a caricature."

Brew looked across to where Gil was engaged in conversation with Mrs Lambert and inwardly smiled. As well to engage the mother when there was no getting near Amabel. It seemed his friend was indeed serious about her. Turning back to Harriet, he smiled quizzically. "You are a woman of strong opinions, are you not?"

"I hope so. Of course, nothing can compare with a man wearing his regimentals."

Her smile faded, and he was only too aware that her thoughts were of her lost love.

"Does it pain you still?"

Harriet brushed her cheek before looking at Brew directly once more. "Does it show so much? No, I cannot in all truth say that John is constantly in my thoughts. It was the talk of uniforms that made me think of him. It is more a dull ache. Forgive me. You surely did not seek me out to talk about things that are long past."

"The war is as much a part of my past as it is yours. Would you like me to tell you what I knew of John Downing? It must have been difficult for those who remained at home in their drawing rooms to imagine what it was like on the battlefield."

Harriet looked at him eagerly. "People do not talk of it. It isn't considered polite conversation in company."

"There is little enough I can say. Our paths only crossed a few times, but each time he conducted himself in a way that honoured him and his uniform. I didn't see him on that fateful day, but I have little doubt the same would have been the case."

"I am grateful to you even for this. The worst thing has always been the awful silence that surrounds circumstances such as mine." There was a terrible sadness about her as she continued. "It isn't only our fighting men who had to be brave. It takes another kind of courage to be left behind."

Brew could have kicked himself for stirring up Harriet's worst memories and apologised quietly, asking if she would like to be left alone. Her mood changed immediately as she broke into a smile.

"Hardly alone with a room full of people. No, please do not go. I might else have to endure another assault from our fine gentleman who casts you all into the shade. Perhaps we can talk some more when we are able to enjoy the promised drive. I cannot tell you how disappointed both Amabel and I were when we looked out of our window this morning."

"No more than I and Mr Carstairs were," Brew answered, picking up on her change of mood. "Ah, it seems I shall have to give up my place after all. Another admirer is bearing down upon you. I will take my leave and look forward to seeing you again soon."

Brew crossed the room to pay his respects to their hostess, though he was always uncomfortable moving in a confined space where people were milling around. It was when he felt at his most vulnerable, for his stick proved to be more of an encumbrance than an aid.

"My compliments, Mrs Lambert. It would seem that, as well as the gentlemen, even the young ladies don't object to coming out in these atrocious conditions when they can be assured of such a welcome as you give them. I trust you are enjoying your time in London."

"Indeed I am, Major Ware. My daughter Harriet would profess that she prefers the quiet of the country, but there is no doubt Amabel is enjoying her first taste of society."

"Both do you proud. I hope you will not object if I call again. In the meantime, I shall do my very best to rearrange a time to take the ladies out in my carriage. Now I must take Mr Carstairs away. Where is he? Ah, he is talking to Miss Amabel. Dare I interrupt, do you think?"

Louisa Lambert smiled knowingly but made no reply.

Brew bore his friend off and on the way back to Grosvenor Square, Gil complained, "I had barely ten minutes to converse with her. Could we not have stayed longer?"

"You will have ample opportunity to pursue your acquaintance when we go for a drive. In the meantime, I am of the opinion that Mrs Lambert looks kindly upon you."

"No! Really? What did she say?"

"Oh, nothing of great moment, but her glance was approving when she looked in your direction."

Gil brightened up immediately, and by the time they reached home he was in a much better frame of mind. Brew, having had ample time to think about the news he had received earlier, took Gil into the library to show him his mother's letter. He sat in silence, watching the fleeting changes of expression on his friend's face as he read.

"You will see her, of course," Gil said at last.

"Of course I shall, and my sister too. As for my father, well, as promised, I tried."

"And that's it? You will make no further effort?"

"What would be the point?"

Gil waved the piece of paper in front of Brew. "This would be the point. What Mrs Ware has said right here. It's none of my business…"

"Then say no more."

"…but you can see how the squire strives still against all the odds. You are a wealthy man. You could help."

Brew felt himself stiffen and his features hardened. He forced his body to relax. Gil only meant well, he knew. He said, much more gently, "He doesn't want my help."

Gil wasn't one to give up easily. "He doesn't know you are in a position to give it. Perhaps if he did, he might be willing."

"You have known my father almost as long as I have. His pride would not allow him to accept anything from me. From anyone. I know your motives are of the finest, and I thank you, but I fear this is beyond mending."

Gil's shoulders sagged in defeat.

"No, don't look like that, old boy. Without your encouragement I would not have written, and I would have been denied the prospect of meeting with my mother and sister. For that I have you to thank. And to show my gratitude, we shall go to White's this evening and you will be treated to the most sumptuous meal they have to offer. How about it?"

"I wonder what I should wear?"

"You are such a dandy!" The atmosphere relaxed as both broke into spontaneous laughter.

CHAPTER FIVE

The weather did not brighten during the ensuing days but Gil had no cause to be disappointed, having the opportunity on several occasions to meet Amabel at some function or other and finding himself fortunate in securing her hand for a number of dances. He was openly pursuing her now and received all the encouragement he could wish for from her fond Mama, who had judged him to be a desirable match for her young daughter.

What Amabel thought herself Louisa did not know, having sufficient sense not to enquire. Well brought up as she was, her daughter showed no preference for any of her suitors, treating all with the same open and friendly manner. Harriet could have enlightened their parent had she chosen to do so, for Amabel had bounced into her room when they'd returned home one evening and, with sparkling eyes, had asked if she did not think Mr Carstairs entirely charming. She was rewarded with a laugh and a raised eyebrow.

"Entirely? There was nothing charming about the manner in which he edged Mr Fanshaw out of the way just as the poor young man was about to solicit your hand," Harriet teased, head on one side.

"Was it not well done, Harry? He confided that he was so anxious to lead me to the floor that he could not bear the thought of another doing so in his stead."

"Yes, he is certainly accomplished."

Amabel's face dropped. "Do you not like him?"

"No, my love, you misunderstand me," Harriet said with a chuckle. "I thought his impatience very appealing. Do you like him so much?"

Amabel blushed. "I do, Harry. Even though I know it is too soon to be forming an attachment, I cannot help that my heart turns over every time I see him."

"There is no need for you to look so mournful. He is receiving enough support from Mama for me to believe she would consider it a fitting alliance."

"I had not expected to enjoy myself nearly as much when we came to London," Amabel said, dancing out of the room again in a world of her own.

Harriet too had had no such expectation. Perhaps time had laid its healing hand upon her. She was finding that whenever she thought of John it was with a gentle fondness, but the despair she'd been carrying had long ago abated. She was much calmer now, enough that she was enjoying the company of other men, specifically Major Brew Ware, she had to admit. She was honest enough to acknowledge, to herself at least, that she found she was looking for him at each engagement and was disappointed when he did not appear. She felt comfortable in his presence. He seemed happy to converse with her in a friendly way that put no pressure upon her. To have found a confidant was the last thing she had anticipated, but she was more than content to have it so.

Brew was playing a close hand. He could not deny that he was attracted to Miss Lambert, but she had given him no reason to be encouraged. He accepted that it was something of a relief to her to be able to talk of John Downing, and he had no doubt her heart still belonged to her deceased fiancé. Well, he was accustomed to keeping his feelings in check, and if he could do no more than make her life a little easier, it would be an honour for him to do so.

He was increasingly preoccupied by the imminent arrival of his family. Gil had learned through his mother that Squire and Mrs Ware, together with their daughter, would be staying in Duke Street and were expected to arrive the next day. Brew was in a quandary. Anxious as he was to see his mother and sister, he was by no means ready to run the risk of happening upon his father unexpectedly. Nor would it be appropriate or desirable to rely on a chance meeting at some function. He had no knowledge as to their intentions. Was there going to be a ball held in Rebecca's honour, or would they be easing her into society gently by other means? They had little if any acquaintance in the capital; Sarah and Matthew Carstairs were possibly the only people they knew well. It therefore stood to reason that Brew's mother might find it difficult to assemble enough guests to make a successful occasion. The more he thought about it, the more he realised that on no account must their first encounter be in the company of strangers. He turned to Gil for help.

"Find out from your mother, if you are able, what my parents' intentions are when they come to town. I must do what I can to avoid any confrontation with my father."

Gil came up trumps. "No problem. I shall ask my father to invite yours to his club and to let me know when that shall be. I am certain he will be keen to do what he can to help in such an awkward situation."

"Excellent! Thank you, Gil. You cannot know how grateful I am."

All that was left to do then was for Brew to wait for a signal from Matthew Carstairs.

Armed with the knowledge that his father would be away from home, Brew paid a visit to Duke Street and remained in the hall as his card was sent up. When he was given a signal by the footman to proceed, his grip, tight on the banister as he climbed the stairs, had little to do with his disability. He entered the drawing room to find his mother already standing, her body rigid with apprehension. It was enough to cause him to relax, and he moved towards her with one hand outstretched.

"Mama! Forgive me."

There was no time for more. He was gathered into her embrace, the stick lying forgotten on the floor as he flung his arms around her. He waited for her sobs to subside before moving back and holding her shoulders.

"I am a scoundrel to have distressed you so. Come, sit down and compose yourself and then we shall talk."

He became aware of a young woman standing by the curtains, an odd smile playing about her lips. He hadn't noticed her on first entering the room but she was unmistakably his sister, though not the Rebecca he remembered. When last he had seen her, she had been a thirteen-year-old child. Before him today stood a beautiful young woman, her blonde hair as thick as his own but nowhere near as unruly. He calculated her now to be twenty years old.

"Becca!"

She came to him, her tears matching his own as he at last allowed his emotions to surface. "My, what a handsome brother I have. But what is this?" she asked, bending to retrieve his walking aid. "A souvenir of the war?"

Brew led her to a chair next to his mother and seated himself opposite them. "Yes, but it was honourably earned."

"I make no doubt of it," his mother said. "Matthew Carstairs has assured me he will keep your father away for at least two hours, so let us make the most of this opportunity. There is much to discuss. Tell us what you can and what you have been doing since the end of the war. The little information we have is from Sarah and Matthew, through Gil, and I must tell you I hung upon their every word."

Brew made as if to speak and then laughed scathingly. "I hardly know where to begin. Let us go back then to that dreadful day in 1803."

Elizabeth Ware drew a sharp breath and he realised he had perhaps been too abrupt.

"It is where it all started, after all. Bear with me if you can, and I will try to explain what I felt and how those feelings had such a significant effect upon my future actions."

Elizabeth nodded and Rebecca took her mother's hand in hers.

"You will remember, Becca, we each made a wish and that Nancy scrambled up, almost tumbling headlong into the well. It would never have occurred to her had I not suggested it, but I was mad for the army and at ten years of age I was willing to try anything to achieve my goal. Even something as ludicrous as casting my wish into a well."

"I remember watching you from the window," Elizabeth said quietly. "Thinking how your father would never be in a position to grant any of you your heart's desire, for it was obvious to me what you were doing. I was as sad for him as for you. He worked so hard to make ends meet, but it was a battle that could not be won."

"Even then I knew he would never be able to purchase a commission for me. But let us not run ahead of ourselves. I realised immediately that the well was dangerous and begged my father to have it covered. That he had insufficient time to do so before the tragic incident we already know, and the next day little Nancy went back. We will none of us ever know why but she had so much spirit in her, and perhaps there was something else she wished to ask for." He paused as all three took some time to reflect. "I screamed at my father, blaming him for not securing the danger. But my anger at him was only a mirror of what I felt towards myself. Had I not shown her the well, she would be with us still. I could not cope and said things I have regretted to this day. Papa was so overcome with grief that he too said words that would have been better left unspoken." It was the first time Brew had referred to Cornelius Ware as Papa in fifteen years. "He blamed me for showing Nancy the way. How could he not, when I blamed myself? Each of us was so white with rage that a chasm was formed that has never been bridged. I had hoped, when at last I wrote … but it is evident he has not forgiven me."

Unaware that he had been leaning forward, Brew sat back in his chair and a silence filled the room, broken by a tap on the door. The footman entered with some refreshment, and Rebecca poured the tea before Elizabeth once again addressed her son. "And after that, hardly a word passed between you. But what happened next, Brew? After you left us."

"After that all I could think about was getting away. Naturally there was no question of me doing so at such an age, but I bided my time until I could enlist in the army and was lucky enough to take part in the hostilities. I earned my souvenir at Waterloo," he said, gesturing to his leg.

A look of pain flew across Elizabeth's face. "We learned that you had attained your majority. Did you then find some benefactor to help you?"

"I was lucky enough to be spotted in the line by a high ranking officer who took me under his wing. He was instrumental in promoting my career and I shall be forever grateful to him."

It was Rebecca's turn to interpose. "The war has been over for nigh on three years, Brew. We know, again from the Carstairs family, that you remained abroad until recently. Were you hospitalised?"

"Only for a short time. My injury was never so bad as to prevent me from being mobile once the initial healing had taken place. No, I stayed because I had nowhere to come home to. Forgive me, Mama," he added as her tears began to flow once more. "I could not return to Austerly. I had my soldier's pay but little else to live on. The war had been my life. I had no desire to remain in my post once it was over." He paused again and a mischievous smile transformed his features, causing another intake of breath from his mother. "The war wasn't all fighting. There were times when we would have been bored out of our minds had it not been for a pack of cards. I became quite proficient. To such an extent, in fact, that I used my skill to earn my living. Don't laugh, Mama, nor you, Becca. I am an extremely wealthy man. I lay odds you never expected to hear that from a Ware!"

They looked at him, obviously stunned at this revelation, and he enjoyed the moment, his charming smile once more in evidence.

"Tell me now about your visit. Do you plan to hold a ball for Rebecca?"

"The funds do not permit of such an extravagance and, in any event, we are acquainted with so few people I should be hard-pressed to know whom to invite. We will make our way gently and are certainly not planning anything of a large nature," Elizabeth said, her smile so like that of her son. "We owe more gratitude than I can say to Sarah and Matthew Carstairs. They are holding a soirée the evening after next, with the express purpose of introducing Rebecca to some of their acquaintance."

"Yes, I am aware. I too have been invited. You will forgive me, both of you, if I do not attend on this occasion. It is inevitable that I should at some stage meet Papa, but I would not have you constrained by fear of a confrontation. It would be just as telling were we to ignore one another entirely, so until you find your feet I shall remain in the background if I can."

"Oh, Brew, I would so love to have you by my side. And naturally I am excited, but filled also with trepidation. My big brother would be such a comfort to me. In spite of that, I can perfectly understand your reasoning." There was irritation in Rebecca's voice. "Surely this estrangement has gone on long enough!"

"It would seem our father doesn't think so, Becca. Until he can be brought to change his mind, if indeed he can, we must tread softly. It would not do your own cause any good if we were seen to be at odds."

"My cause?"

"But of course, my darling sister. Did you not confide in me that your wish was for a handsome prince?" Brew said, the ready smile springing to his face.

Elizabeth looked from son to daughter. "A prince?"

"Why yes, Mama. In those days I wanted only to rescue my father from the poverty that was obvious to me, even at so young an age. I could not bear to see him worry so."

"And you thought a prince would be the answer to your prayers, did you? Yes, I can see a child might believe it to be so. Sadly, real life isn't like that. If I could but see you comfortably joined with a man whom you could love, I would be happy. The worry of inheriting an estate that brings with it no means of maintaining it soon drives a wedge between the most devoted of people."

Elizabeth's voice faded into the silence as her children realised, as they never had before, that their mother's life had been every bit as hard as the squire's.

Brew took her hand, pressing it gently. "Did you not love my father, Mama?"

She looked up, her eyes brimming with tears, and a strange smile lightened her features. "Love him? Oh yes, Brew. Such a handsome young man he was, not unlike yourself, and with a sense of fun that you would now find it hard to believe."

Neither argued with her.

"It was the burden, you see. Pride would not let him sell the home that had been in his family for generations. We could have lived more discreetly in a far smaller property, but Cornelius wouldn't hear of it. He was the squire. There was a position to maintain. As time passed, he grew more frustrated and withdrawn. It was not only you, my darlings, from whom he became aloof. After Nancy..." Her voice broke on the word and she tried again. "After Nancy, the distance between us became a barrier I have never been able to breach. Your father is a lonely and bitter man. Had it not been for you, Becca, my life would have been insupportable. No, don't, Brew," she said as her son snatched his hand away and jumped up, pacing the room awkwardly. There was anguish in Elizabeth's eyes as she watched the unevenness of his gait and saw him grasp the back of a chair for support. "Yours was not the blame. You were only a child. In the end it was better, perhaps, that you did go away. My only recrimination is that you did not stay in touch. I worried about you so, you see."

Brew flung himself at her feet and looked up into her face, tears streaming from his eyes. She stroked his hair, just as she had when he was a child.

"There, there. It's over now. We are together again and the terrible pride that separated us is cast aside. I think perhaps it is time for you to go. I'm anxious, for your father may return sooner than anticipated. I leave it to you to make such arrangements as you are able so that we three may meet again soon. You may have been estranged from one parent for most of your life, but believe me when I say that I never blamed you for what happened. I pray only that the time will come when you can forgive yourself."

Brew took some moments, striving for calm. Himself once more, he kissed his mother and his sister before smiling playfully at Rebecca and saying, "I hope you find your prince, my dear." And with that, he was gone.

CHAPTER SIX

The weather smiled kindly upon Brew and Gil the following day. The Lambert ladies, having no other pressing engagement, responded in the affirmative to the hastily written note enquiring if they were free to join the gentlemen for the promised drive. Having given her permission for her daughters to go, Louisa rang the bell in the drawing room, where they had been sitting at their different occupations. Amabel was flicking through the pages of the latest fashions, Louisa was sewing, and Harriet was sitting in the window seat, reading a book. A footman soon appeared at the door in response to the bell.

Louisa looked up. "Trevor, would you be good enough to convey a message to cook for me? I should like a picnic hamper to be assembled as soon as can be and conveyed to the hall in an hour. And Trevor," she continued with an engaging smile as the footman was bowing himself out of the room, "please apologise to her on my behalf for the short notice. I know how busy she is."

"A picnic hamper, Mama? In March?"

"But it is very mild, you will agree, Harriet. It would be a shame indeed to forego the opportunity," Louisa said with a swift glance at Amabel.

Harriet bit her lip in an effort not to smile. What a scheming person Mama was. Well, she was happy enough to go along. She had been no older than her sister when she had fallen so deeply in love with John Downing. Her short-lived happiness had been snatched from her, and she would throw no rub in the way of promoting Amabel's hopes.

The sisters had ample opportunity to prepare themselves before the allotted time, and Amabel changed her attire not once but twice. Harriet was outwardly much calmer about the forthcoming treat, but a frisson of excitement nestled just below the surface. She didn't question it, merely preparing herself for a day she felt certain she would enjoy.

From the window, Harriet saw a smart-looking carriage draw up outside, pulled by four horses. Gil was shown into the room, Brew having waited with his team, and he was profuse in his thanks when Louisa informed him of the hamper that they were to take with them. It gave them the option to drive out of town, rather than in the park.

Brew's tiger, Walter, held the horses' heads while his master handed Harriet up into the front seat, Amabel and Gil sitting behind them. The rugs which had been brought for their comfort were laid over their knees, for even though the temperature was far higher than was usual for the time of year, it would not do to risk catching a chill. The picnic hamper was loaded and they were off, Walter letting go the bridle and jumping nimbly up behind as the equipage pulled away. Progress was slow to begin with, they not being the only ones to take advantage of the change in the weather. After some expert manoeuvring through the traffic until the road lay clear in front of them, Brew was able to turn his attention more easily to his companion.

"That is a very attractive bonnet you are wearing, Miss Lambert. I trust it will remain firmly in place if I give the horses their heads. They are keen to get going, I can tell you."

"You don't seem to have any difficulty in holding them, sir. And you surprise me. I didn't take you for one to be giving empty compliments."

Brew laughed out loud. She enjoyed the sound of it.

"No, ma'am, you do me an injustice. I would rather keep my tongue between my teeth than make such comments as are not genuine. It is a very fetching confection, the brim framing your face and bringing out the colour in your eyes. You should always wear green."

Harriet chuckled in response. "You are outrageous, Major Ware, as well as accomplished. It is evident you have some experience of such things. Save your pretty remarks for those who might be flattered by them."

His smile turned to a frown and he glanced at her, his expression serious, before turning his attention back to the road. "I meant no flattery. How could you think so? You cannot be unaware of your beauty."

Harriet was at a loss as to what to say next. She had, up to this point, always been perfectly comfortable in Brew's company. He had never before put her to the blush and she didn't know how to deal with it. Inside her muff her hands were clenched together, and it wasn't on account of the cold. Fortunately for both of them, Gil called from behind.

"Come on, old man, the road ahead is clear. Time to spring 'em."

"It is ever neck or nothing with you, Carstairs. As you wish. We must rely on the ladies not to tell their mother that the sedate drive she thought they were taking was anything but," Brew said, and he set off at a spanking pace. By the time he'd drawn the horses into a walk again, the uncomfortable moment had passed and Harriet was able to relax once more.

Following Gil's instructions, Brew had set off in a northerly direction from Hay Hill. They travelled as far as the village of Hampstead before it was decided by mutual consent that they should go no further until they had addressed the picnic that had been prepared for them.

"Turn right up ahead, old boy, and I shall direct you to a suitable place."

A perfect spot was found and rugs were laid on the ground for them to sit on. Gil placed the picnic basket in the middle and Brew leaned down and removed some items for Walter, in whose charge they had left the horses. When he joined them again, he sat down a little awkwardly and Harriet recollected his impediment. She was certain the last thing he would want was to be reminded of it and so she turned to Gil who was offering her a plate which he had loaded rather generously. She laughed and thanked him, saying she would do her best but she rather thought it would be beyond her. Then, as he did the same for Amabel, Harriet turned to Brew. "That was kind of you."

For a moment he looked puzzled and then the smile which she had learned to expect of him spread across his features. She liked that she never had to explain to him what she meant.

"Would you have me leave the poor fellow in the cold with nothing for his comfort?"

"It is cold, isn't it?" she replied with a chuckle. "I think perhaps Mama was a little optimistic when she provided a meal for us to eat out of doors."

"But so generous of her. Will they make a match of it, those two, do you think?" he said in an undertone. Amabel and Gil were so lost in their own conversation that they didn't heed what their companions were saying.

"I hope so. I was as young myself when I met John. I think it no bad thing to meet one's chosen partner in life at an early age."

Brew briefly occupied himself with eating his sandwich before turning to his friend. "You have chosen a good spot here, Gil, but I fear the ladies are becoming chilled. What say you we find a hostelry, hopefully one with a fire?"

"Chilled! Good heavens, no," Harriet said with an exaggerated shiver but laughing all the same. "This tremor is one I have been afflicted with since childhood, and I scarce give it any heed."

"Enough! Escort the ladies back to the carriage, Gil, and I will deal with this," Brew said, waving a hand over the remnants of their meal before giving Harriet his hand to help her rise. She liked the warmth and the strength of it. The picnic was packed away and Harriet, watching Brew surreptitiously, was happy to see that he managed well enough in spite of his injury.

Mr Carstairs, familiar with the area, took them to The Spaniards Inn close by and they were glad indeed to find a fire roaring in the hearth. He delighted the ladies with tales of the highwayman, Dick Turpin. "He was known to frequent this place," he said. "He was very famous around these parts, I can tell you. Executed him in the end, they did, poor fellow."

Amabel's eyes opened wide, and she glanced over her shoulder and shivered.

"No need for you to be in a worry, though. There's no question of his ghost walking here. He'd moved to Yorkshire by then."

"His ghost!"

Harriet laughed at her sister. "He's roasting you, my dear. Don't encourage him." And to Gil, "You should be ashamed of yourself, frightening her like that."

"I swear I shall not sleep a wink tonight, Mr Carstairs," said Amabel, but she too was laughing.

Brew, conscious of the time, suggested that perhaps they should leave else it would be growing dark before they arrived back in Hay Hill. There was little conversation on the journey home, all four companions content to enjoy the drive, and the Misses Lambert were handed over to their mama just as the light was fading.

"Will you not come in for some refreshment, gentlemen?" Louisa asked them, but they declined, merely saying that they hoped to have the honour of repeating the experience again in the near future.

"I hope to see you at my parents' soirée tomorrow evening, ma'am," Gil said.

"I shall look forward to it. And you, Major Ware, will you too be there?"

"Unfortunately not, Mrs Lambert. I am going out of town for a few days and will be unable to attend."

Harriet, standing by, was at pains not to let him see her disappointment. She had, these last weeks, taken so much pleasure in his company that she now acknowledged to herself that she would miss him. At least she would know not to look for him. She and Amabel once again thanked them for a lovely day and waved as they mounted the carriage and left.

"Out of town, Brew?" Gil asked as they drove away. "I had no notion. Where are you off to, then?"

"My father is settled in London for a while. I believe it's time for me to go back to Austerly."

The idea had come upon Brew quite suddenly. Though there were many things he might have occupied himself with in town, he realised it would be an opportunity to use the time to advantage. Upon reaching Grosvenor Square, he excused himself to Gil and went into the library to write a letter to his mother.

My dearest Mama

Seeing you and Becca yesterday served to impress upon me how very much I have missed you both. Not only that, but Austerly too. While much of my childhood was unhappy (forgive me, Mama, but we all know it to be true) it was and is still my home, and there are fond memories also which time has not erased.

Until I can hit upon a way of resolving my father's implacability, I fear I will serve only as an embarrassment to my sister if I run the risk of meeting you all together in public. I have decided therefore to journey north for a few days. While you are not in residence I won't, out of respect, stay at the house but will find accommodation nearby. Austerly is not yet mine but it will be one day, and I feel no compunction in visiting the estate to see how the land lies. It will, after all, become my responsibility in due course and, while I would not dream of enquiring into financial circumstances that are currently none of my business, it may be that I will be able to see my way clear as to what I might achieve when the time comes.

Though I have not yet done so, I will ask Gil Carstairs to engage a box for me so that I may, if you wish, take you and Becca to the theatre upon my return to London. But more of that later. Meanwhile, it is my intention to leave early in the morning. My hope is that this letter finds you in Duke Street and that you will have sufficient time to charge me with any errands you may wish me to carry home. If you have none, I shall contact you again when I have accomplished my journey.

Your loving son
Brew

His body alive with new purpose, Brew rang the bell and asked for his letter to be delivered and that François join him immediately in the library. The valet, on being informed that they would be travelling in the morning and being asked to assemble such clothes as his master might require for a week in the country, became exceedingly voluble. Brew, accustomed to his histrionics, allowed him a few minutes to address his grievances at being given so little notice. He then threatened to go without him if he was going to make such a fuss and dismissed him with a wave of the hand.

"Go without me, monsieur!" François expostulated. "And who, may I enquire, would look after your boots and present you just as you wish, *comme ça*?" He gestured toward Brew. "*C'est moi qui le fais*!" With which parting shot he left the room.

Gil, entering in his wake, wanted to know what his friend was laughing at.

"Nothing, dear boy, nothing at all. Only that I have once again upset my valet. But he's damned good and I admit I would be lost without him, though I wouldn't tell him that, of course."

"You don't have to, old man. He knows already. Came to ask if you fancied dining at White's this evening. I've a mind to go there myself."

"A fitting end to a most enjoyable day. Let us hope that I can mollify François sufficiently that he is prepared to come down off the ropes and do his best by me."

"Never a doubt. He has his pride to consider. Shall we say in an hour?"

Only a little more than the designated time later the two friends set off arm in arm. The weather, though a trifle chilly, was clement enough not to necessitate taking a hackney. Brew was dressed in his usual black and silver and Gil somewhat more flamboyantly, but the turnout of both was immaculate. Their evening garments were concealed beneath the protective cloaks they wore in anticipation of a sharp drop in temperature as the hour advanced. The gas lighting was sufficient to show them the way and their pace was leisurely, neither being in a hurry and Gil not wishing to discomfort his companion.

They were perhaps three dozen paces from their destination when they observed two older men descending the steps of White's and turning up St James's Street in their direction. The gentlemen in question were well known to both younger men. Gil was about to hail his father when Brew's grip tightened on his arm, for Matthew Carstairs' companion was none other than Cornelius Ware. Even in the dim light, Brew was able to see clearly how haggard his parent had become since last he had seen him. He halted, and Gil with him, and had begun to step forward again when the squire looked directly at him and crossed the road, taking Carstairs with him. Gil's father, obviously caught unawares, had time only to doff his hat at his son and his friend before being led away.

"Well, if that don't beat all," Gil said, watching as the other two moved away, one of them without a backward glance. "You know what I think, don't you?"

"No, but I'm sure you're going to tell me," said Brew, his gaze following his father's retreating figure.

"I think we should get drunk."

"Happy to oblige, old boy. Happy to oblige."

Brew awoke the following morning with little recollection of the night before, Gil having done his job well. One thing, though, he could not forget. There had been a complete lack of emotion on his father's face before he had turned away from his only son. A rage filled him such as he had not known for many a year. It wasn't helped by a note from his mother that had been delivered the previous evening, when he'd been in no state to read it. François brought it to his bedchamber now with some hot chocolate, which beverage Brew looked at in horror and refused to drink.

"Now then, monsieur, you know we have a long day ahead of us," François pleaded, his passionate burst of emotion of the previous day forgotten in the concern he had for his master.

"Either you will take it away or I will pour it over your head!"

The valet retired, defeated, and Brew tore open his mother's note.

My dearest boy

I have no particular messages for you to carry home, though it was kind indeed of you to ask. The theatre sounds like a delightful idea. Becca was very excited when I told her of your plan.

It is perhaps as well that you will be absent for a while. Your father came home this evening in what I can only describe as a foul mood. I know not why, but it would be better not to risk the two of you meeting at present.

Do not stay away for too long. I miss you already.
Mama

Brew sighed. He could have enlightened his mother. He rather fancied his father's mood was no more foul than his own.

Two hours later he was ready to leave, his carriage waiting for him at the door. Remembering to ask Gil about arranging to hire a box in Drury Lane, he climbed inside, settling himself down in the corner and wishing he were riding, for his mind would then be occupied elsewhere. Instead, he sank his chin on his chest and tried to ignore the effects of the previous evening's excesses. As his valet had so rightly predicted, it was going to be a long day.

CHAPTER SEVEN

Although Harriet was enjoying her social life once more, there had been a slight diminishing of enthusiasm after she had learned that Major Ware was not going to be attending the Carstairs family's soirée. However, she went willingly enough and neither her mother nor her sister would have been able to discern any change in her.

She and her family had no idea as to the degree of curiosity consuming their hostess, for it was at her son's instigation that Sarah had invited the Lamberts to attend. So out of character was this that, by no means dull-witted, it was inevitable she would arrive at the obvious conclusion. What she didn't know was which of the two young ladies had engaged Gil's enthusiasm. Having despaired of trying to fix his interest with any of the girls she had deemed desirable as a wife for her son, she was more than a little apprehensive that his eye might have fallen upon someone entirely unsuitable. What, after all, did she know of this family? She had not met them at the time of the elder daughter's come out, for she had not visited town at all that year and she knew little of them except that the mother was a widow.

She mentioned nothing of this to her husband, who had on several occasions said to her, "Leave the boy alone. It will happen in his own time." Sarah had no great belief in destiny and felt the need to give it a little help from time to time. Well, it seemed that on this occasion Matthew had been right, and it didn't take more than a minute for her to discover which of the sisters was the object of Gil's affection. And she was delighted. Amabel was a pretty girl with delightful manners.

She was vivacious without being forward and thanked Mrs Carstairs very prettily for inviting her. When she moved along the line to greet her son, there was a marked change in her and even more so in Gil. Sarah was able to observe them out of the corner of her eye while welcoming her next guest. Gil was always charming. An affable young man, he was happy in any company or, if not, certainly gentleman enough not to show it. She had never had reason to be anything but excessively proud of him. But the way he greeted the younger Miss Lambert indicated that this was something very different indeed. He bowed over her hand and looked up into her eyes as he did so. His mother could not be mistaken. She felt a constriction in her throat and experienced a strong desire to get to know this young woman better.

Shortly after the arrival of Louisa and her daughters came that of Squire and Mrs Ware, together with their daughter, Rebecca. Both Sarah and her husband greeted these old friends and neighbours with enthusiasm and, as the main purpose of the evening was to present Miss Ware to the ton, she was at pains to introduce her to the assembled company. It wasn't until some while later that she was able to engage with the Lamberts. They were seated with Rebecca and her mother, with Gil in attendance. A quick glance around the room reassured her that none of her guests was without company or attention.

Sarah walked towards the group seated on the window side of the attractive room which she had caused to be refurbished only the year before, having grown tired of the red curtains and furnishings and preferring instead a pale blue, which she found much easier on the eye. A patterned carpet covered the floor, predominantly the same colour as the drapes, and the effect was altogether to her satisfaction.

Gil rose from his chair as his mother approached and offered it to her, if a little reluctantly. She smiled inwardly and sent him off to get some drinks for, although the night air might be cold outside, the saloon was warm enough to give anyone a thirst. He went obligingly and Sarah turned first to the two matrons, the three younger women being seated on her other side. Cornelius Ware was nowhere to be seen and she assumed he must be in the card room.

"It is such a pleasure to meet you, Mrs Lambert. My son tells me he made your acquaintance but recently."

"That is true, yes, and I must thank you again for inviting us here this evening. It has been some three years since we were last in London and it is like a breath of fresh air to be returning, it being time to launch Amabel into the world. And Mrs Ware tells me that is her purpose too in coming to town with Miss Ware. Is that not so, Mrs Ware?" she asked, addressing the other.

"Assuredly it is. I should have no idea how to go on if it weren't for my friend Sarah here, for the squire and I live quite a secluded life in Lincolnshire. We are neighbours there, you understand."

"The girls seem to be getting on very well, don't you think?" Louisa said, glancing across to where all three were deep in animated conversation. "It can be uncomfortable to be among strangers," she went on, continuing this theme but in no way exerting any pressure. "Perhaps, if you permit, my daughters and I might pay you a morning visit so they may become better acquainted, particularly if Miss Ware has few acquaintances in London."

"I should be delighted to see you all. The squire is not much at home, taking the opportunity while we are here to accompany Mr Carstairs to his club and all those other places where gentlemen choose to spend so much of their time."

It seemed to Sarah that this first evening was going remarkably well, for which she was naturally excessively pleased. A delightful lady with much the same happy outlook on life as her son, she could only be satisfied at the success of Rebecca's first outing, for several of those present had engaged with her during the evening. In addition, a long-awaited dream looked as if it might at last become a reality with the entry onto the scene of the younger Miss Lambert.

Two very tedious days after leaving London, with every bone in his body aching and his injured leg paining him, Brew arrived in the vicinity of Austerly and elected to stay at The Bertie Arms in Uffington. Its warm-coloured stone and thatch roof were the most welcoming things he had seen since leaving town, for he knew it marked the end of his journey. Naturally it was not a place he had visited as a child, nor had he been there even as a youth, and he was therefore by sight unknown to the landlord, who introduced himself as Packham. Consequently Brew was somewhat taken aback when that worthy, on having his visitor's identity made known to him, welcomed him warmly in a manner far in excess of what might have been expected for a casual traveller.

"What a pleasure it is to have you back in these parts, Major. You'll doubtless be wanting your dinner. If you'll excuse me, I'll go and see what my wife can rustle up for you and arrange for the best bedchamber to be made ready," Packham said, carefully folding Brew's cloak over his arm and bowing himself out with a smile. He was back only a few moments later with some liquid sustenance and showed a tendency to linger, enquiring with due deference as to whether they might be privileged to see more of him now he was home. He busied himself making up the fire as he spoke and Brew, thinking only of his stomach and longing for his bed, kindly but firmly put him out of the room.

In far less time than he would have believed possible, a not inconsiderable meal was placed before him and the major unhurriedly worked his way through it. Having sent for some port, he asked Packham to convey his compliments to his good lady and settled down in a chair in front of the fire, his heels placed comfortably on a footstool. He soon decided, however, that it would be advisable to retire before such time as he fell asleep where he sat. The landlord showed him to his room, where François had already unpacked his things and was waiting to help him out of his coat and pull off his boots. This he did before Brew said, "I can manage very well without you now. If you are even half as tired as I am, you will be more than ready to seek your couch."

"Certainly, if monsieur requires nothing more?"

"Go to bed, François, for that is what I shall be doing before many more minutes have passed." The grin that accompanied his words took away any offence the valet might have felt at not being allowed to see his master attired for the night and between the sheets. He left, carrying the boots with him.

Brew snuffed the candle and lay on his back, hands clasped behind his head as he stared at the ceiling. He had left the curtains open, a habit he had acquired since his army days, preferring the feeling of openness it always gave. The moon was close to full and the room was illuminated such that he could see every detail. His attention moved from the ceiling to a small stand upon which rested a jug and wash basin. Against another wall there was a chest of drawers, next to which his portmanteau had been placed, and a wardrobe too in which he had no doubt his clothes were now neatly arranged. He raised his eyes again. They remained stubbornly open. With a sigh he got out of bed and stepped across to the window. He gazed out, not focusing, aware that Austerly was only a short distance from where he stood.

Home, he thought. *After all these years I am home.* With that, he returned to his bed and was at last able to fall into a deep and dreamless sleep.

Eager yet apprehensive, Brew took his time over breakfast the following morning. He had asked Packham to arrange for the hire of a hack, hoping optimistically that he would not be provided with a broken-down nag. His trust was not misplaced and a fine bay horse was saddled and waiting for him. He left the inn, telling the landlord as he went that he had no idea what time he would return but to keep his room for him.

"I shall assuredly be coming back," he said. "And I should be obliged to your good lady if she will once again provide me with dinner."

Reassured on that head, he delayed no longer. As he approached the gates to Austerly, he found that his heart was pumping hard. The property was set some few hundred yards back from the road, an old house of mixed architectural styles, for there had been additions over time which gave it a rambling effect. It stood three storeys high with mullioned windows in the centre section that formed the original structure. In the sunlight he could see that some effort had been made to tend the gardens to the front of the building, but there was still a neglected look about them, and to the house itself.

Dismounting and securing the horse's reins to a post which stood to one side, he retrieved his stick, which he had previously attached to the saddle. Taking a deep breath, Major Benedict Richmond Edward Ware climbed the front steps to the door of his childhood home. He rapped the knocker and waited. When there was no response after two or three minutes, he repeated the action, putting more strength behind it, and this time there was a result. He heard a bolt being pulled aside and the door was dragged backwards.

For Brew it was as if time fell away as he looked upon the face of William Kettersham, the old butler. His back was more bent than in years gone by but he stood proud as ever until, recognising the surprise visitor, tears welled in his eyes and he so far forgot himself as to step forward and embrace the squire's heir.

"Master Benedict, Master Benedict. Is it really you? Come in, sir. Come in and I shall fetch Pru, for she will be irked with me indeed if I don't let her know immediately that you have come home."

It was not however necessary for his childhood nurse to be summoned, for she too had responded to the clamour on the door and appeared in the hallway as Kettersham spoke. His tears were nothing compared to hers and, though Brew stood more than a foot taller than her, she gathered him into her arms as though he were the child she had cared for so long ago.

With Pru's head against his shoulder, Brew looked beyond her and into the hall. It was an impressive edifice and had once been the most admired house in the area. An oak staircase climbed from the centre of the entrance way, dividing as it reached the first floor. The ornate banister spoke of the excellent taste of a long-gone ancestor, the marble floor from which it arose spreading to the left and right and behind the stairs to rooms that were hidden from view by this centrepiece. It had been meant to impress, and impress it did.

But Major Ware saw none of this. As if through a mist, he remembered times when he and his sisters had straddled the balustrade and slid down its polished surface from the landing to the hall below. He heard childish laughter, remembered protecting Becca and Nancy by taking upon himself the blame for the escapade which all knew was forbidden. So long had his memories of this place been coupled with the tragedy of his sister's death and his separation from his father that he had truly forgotten how happy his childhood had been until then. He gave himself a mental shake and put the old nurse away from him, his hands on her shoulders and his eyes smiling into hers.

"Well, Pru, I swear you didn't expect to see me today, did you?"

"You can be sure of that, Master Benedict. We've long wondered, Kettersham and me, if we'd ever set eyes on you again. Isn't that so, William?" she said, addressing the butler who had just closed and bolted the door once more and turned to face them.

He didn't answer Pru's question but said pointedly, "The family is away from home, sir."

"Yes, I am aware. I have seen my mother and my sister in London." Brew had no need to mention the squire. Both these old retainers were well aware of the situation. "Join me, if you will, in my mother's drawing room."

They followed him across the floor to a room that was situated behind the staircase and whose windows looked out onto the garden. He caught sight of the well and felt his stomach churn.

"Sit down and I will explain why I have come at this time."

"Yes, but you'll be wanting your old room to be got ready, and I'll need to speak to Cook about getting something special in for you. She and Mr Gardner are still here."

"Don't trouble yourself, Kettersham. I shall not be staying here. I'm bunking down at The Bertie Arms where I have bespoken dinner for this evening."

"You're not staying here?" Pru asked, obviously amazed and deeply offended.

"Please, sit down and allow me to explain."

They did so and, though neither made any mention of his disability, Brew noticed the pain in his old nurse's eyes as she glanced at his stick. They sat, eyes wide open and waiting expectantly.

"We three have no secrets. How could we, indeed, when it was the two of you who rescued me from so many scrapes in the past and sheltered me from my father? No, I don't ask you to be disloyal to him in any way, but you must know that I wrote to him recently, asking that he contact me. He has chosen not to do so. I know he received my letter, for my mother told me. It has been some time now since I have yearned to come home, though I have only recently returned to England. My father's silence was indication enough that I was not welcome here, but I have the right. Rather than impose myself upon him, I have chosen to come when I am aware he is at present fixed in London."

"He's never been the same since Miss Nancy…" Pru left the sentence unfinished. "Nobody has. We all hoped over the years that he would have that old well demolished, but he never has. Oh, he covered it over all right, we all know that, when you were just a lad. But it's almost as if he leaves it there to remind himself of his pain."

"And what of my mother's pain, looking out on it as she must every time she sits in this room?" Brew demanded. There was anger in his voice and he apologised immediately, assuring them again that he was not there to denigrate his parent. "I come because one day this will be mine," he went on, making a sweeping gesture with his hand. "I am aware that things have gone to rack and ruin, and I do not blame my father for that. He inherited an extensive property but not the means to maintain it. The fault is not his, nor has the remedy been. However, I have the means to put all to rights." For the first time since they had entered the room, he smiled.

"You do?"

"Yes, Pru. Did you think I had come back cap in hand? Nothing like it. I am a very wealthy man." The smile became a grin. "In due course, Austerly will be returned to its former glory. My father knows nothing of this, and without his permission I am unable to begin what I know to be a monumental task. And that is why I have come at this time. With the squire away, I shall have the freedom to examine both house and estate so that I may make plans for the future. While I would prefer to begin now, if only to bring some comfort to my mother — for it must distress her to see everything growing increasingly more shabby — it is not in my power to override my father's wishes. Now, while I go and see my horse stabled, perhaps you could organise some coffee, after which I should like to tour the house."

CHAPTER EIGHT

Mrs Lambert wasted no time in carrying her daughters off to Duke Street the next day and was happy to find Elizabeth and Rebecca Ware at home. Not only that, but Sarah Carstairs was there too, having been escorted by her son. Gil had used the excuse that he wished to pay his respects to his childhood friend, but as he and Rebecca had been in the habit of seeing much of each other on those occasions he had been in Lincolnshire, he wasn't fooling his mother for a moment. She it was who had told him that the Lamberts might possibly be found there in the hope of promoting the attachment between him and Amabel. She was delighted Gil's aspirations had fallen upon such a charming girl and had said as much to her husband that very morning.

"Up to your tricks again, are you?" Matthew asked, gently pinching her cheek. "Well, I hope you may be right. Not that I am in such haste as you to see our son married, but she is well-connected and her manners are unaffected."

"We are planning, he and I, to see Elizabeth and Rebecca later on. Would you care to join us?"

"I will, my dear, but only to bear Cornelius off to my club." He sighed and added, "You have no conception as to how different he is when associating only with men. It's as well he takes little part in the community at home, other than where his duties as squire come into play, for his bearing in mixed company leaves much to be desired. One might almost take him for a block, so tongue-tied does he become. When there are no ladies about, he is quite different."

"How so, dearest?"

"It is certain he'll never be the life and soul of any party, but it seems to me he is more relaxed somehow. It's almost as if he isn't required to wear a face that doesn't fit him."

Sarah was tempted to say more, for her feelings were in stark contrast to those of her spouse. Matthew was a jovial man who took life very much as it came, ready to make allowances where he deemed it necessary, but Elizabeth was a close friend. Though she had confided little to Sarah over the years, it was plain enough that Cornelius's wife received scant support from her husband. Both had suffered the same tragedy and the loss of a child, particularly under such circumstances, was not easy to bear. But Squire Ware had excluded everyone, including Elizabeth, leaving her not just with the loss of a daughter but in some ways of her husband too.

Later, when Brew had left home, she suffered yet another sort of bereavement, and this had been the only time she had broken down in front of her friend. Sarah had done what she could to comfort her when in fact there was really nothing she could do. She remembered well Elizabeth's words when Brew had gone: "I hope he is now satisfied!" They were spoken bitterly and referred, Sarah knew, not to the son but to the husband. It was the only time she had ever uttered a word against him, but there was no doubt in Sarah's mind that the two were estranged, residing under the same roof but living more as acquaintances than as husband and wife.

She said nothing of this to Matthew, only remarking, "As well if you carry him off, then."

This he was not able to do immediately, several of his visitors of the previous evening having gone to Duke Street to further their acquaintance with Elizabeth and Rebecca. By the time he had exchanged pleasantries with them all, Cornelius had left the room. Matthew ran him to earth in the library and could only wish that his neighbour was more able to engage with people. He found his quarry sitting with his head in his hands and was about to retire once more when the squire looked up.

"Come in, Matthew, come in. Sit down for a moment if you will. You must have wondered the other evening why I drew you across the street, away from your son, and from mine."

He paused, but Carstairs was wise enough to make no comment.

"It was the first time I had seen Brew since he left home all those years ago. But it wasn't the first time I had heard from him. He wrote to me a few weeks ago." He looked at Matthew, who maintained his silence. "Told me a bit about his time in the army. Apologised for, well, things in the past. Wanted me to contact him."

"And?" Matthew asked, feeling it was time he made some comment.

"I ignored his letter. I didn't even show it to Elizabeth until much later. And then, seeing him like that, unexpectedly, something in me shut down. Instead of taking the opportunity to heal the rift, I widened it even further by cutting him dead. I thought he might have come to your soirée. That I might have spoken to him then."

Matthew thought Brew had more sense than to walk into the lion's den and so it had proved, for he knew Sarah had invited him.

"Elizabeth has never forgiven me for what I said to him. I laid the blame for Nancy's death upon him, a ten-year-old boy. And now, when at last he has made contact, has apologised, I have hurt him again. I doubt he'll want anything more to do with me." Cornelius pushed his chair back and rose to his feet. He was a tall man, though a little stooped, as much with abjection as with age. "Take me to your club, if you will. Perhaps I can push away my demons for a while in a game of cards."

In the drawing room Rebecca was deep in conversation with Harriet, having no idea of the pain her father was suffering.

"You must excuse me, Miss Lambert, if I seem overly excited. It has been my wish for so long to come to London and I feared it would never happen."

"It is the dream of most young women, I believe. But please, call me Harriet."

"Thank you, if you will call me Becca, for it is what I prefer and far less formal than my given name. Though I must say I am grateful for it because it is my godmother, for whom I was named, who funds this trip."

Harriet was a little surprised at the disclosure of so much information, but she came to the conclusion that Rebecca was much like her brother, frank and open in her ways.

"Then you are truly indebted to her. Does she live in London?"

"No, sadly she passed away two years ago, but she made provision for me in her will. Do you remain long in Hay Hill?"

"We are fixed here for some time. My mother has hired the house for the season to fire off my sister into society. And you?"

"I believe we shall be here for some weeks. I hope we may see much of each other," Becca said.

Harriet found Miss Ware as engaging as her sibling and remarked, "I have recently been introduced to a Major Ware, who I understand is your brother. You are very like him."

"That's right. We met again only recently after many years apart."

"He has been abroad, of course, in the army."

"That isn't the only reason we have been separated. I will tell you all about it, but not here. It is too noisy and there are too many people."

Harriet's curiosity was aroused but at that moment Amabel, who had been for some time in conversation with Gil, approached the two young women and said that Louisa was ready to leave and she had come to tear her sister away. In the carriage, their mama informed her daughters that she had been talking with Sarah Carstairs and Elizabeth Ware and that Sarah had invited them to dine in two days' time. It was to be a small party, made up only of their hosts, the Wares and themselves.

"We shall be an uneven number, Mrs Carstairs informed me, but she explained that it is to be an informal evening," said Louisa. "She seemed not to be concerned about arranging a table where the ladies will outnumber the men and too many people will be related to each other."

Harriet and Amabel both looked forward to the date, the younger by reason of the fact that Gil Carstairs would be there and Harriet because she looked forward to becoming better acquainted with Rebecca Ware.

Harriet had an opportunity to study Cornelius Ware closely, as he was seated diagonally opposite her at the table. She was shocked at his appearance; he seemed rather old to be the parent of Brew and Rebecca. In addition, he gave the impression of being far more advanced in years than his wife beside him, a vivacious woman to whom Harriet had taken an immediate liking. And then he looked up and she thought she had never before seen such pain in someone's eyes. She averted her gaze immediately, wanting neither to appear rude nor to look any longer upon his torment.

Fortunately her attention was commanded by Gil Carstairs, and she was grateful to have something else to occupy her thoughts. He was doing a splendid job as second host. Although Amabel was at his left hand and Harriet knew his inclination was to engage with her, he nonetheless ensured he did not neglect her or indeed any of the other guests. Convention was thrown out of the window as conversation was exchanged not just with one's neighbours but around and across the table. Only the squire, Harriet observed, barely joined in. On Elizabeth's left side at the head of the table was Matthew Carstairs, and they conversed with the ease of long-standing friends. Harriet had little opportunity to talk with Rebecca until the ladies left the gentlemen to their port and adjourned to the drawing room.

"Come and sit beside me, child," Sarah said to Amabel, which she did, sinking onto a stool at her feet. Louisa and Elizabeth joined them, and Sarah unobtrusively watched the young woman whom she now dearly hoped would become her daughter-in-law. On the other side of the room, Harriet and Rebecca sat together and resumed the conversation they had begun two days earlier.

"What a very hospitable couple the Carstairs are. I understand you have known them your whole life," Harriet said, hoping Becca would renew her confidences.

"I think their support was the reason my mother was able to get through each day after Nancy died."

"Nancy?"

"My sister. Fifteen years ago." Her fingers moved restlessly in her lap.

"I'm so sorry. She must have been so young. Some illness, perhaps?"

"It would have been preferable had it been an illness. No, what am I saying? But it was an accident. A horrible accident. And my brother takes the blame upon himself."

Harriet wasn't sure how to proceed. She need not have worried. Becca told her it was a relief to talk about it. It was not discussed at home; it had never been discussed at home, and that in its way reaped its own tragedy, for they were a family in mourning but unable to support each other.

"But let me first tell you what happened. My brother was ten years old and mad for the army. He would have done anything for a commission but he knew our father, when the time came, would never be in a position to fulfil his dream. There is a well which stands at the back of the house and, being a spirited boy, he dragged me and Nancy there one day so we each could make a wish. Children have such vivid imaginations, and though he professed not to believe in such things, I feel sure that in his mind it added to the very remote possibility that one day he would be granted his heart's desire."

"Well, history tells us that he did at least achieve his aim."

"Yes, but at such a cost. I was five at the time and Nancy only four. She wasn't tall enough to reach, but there was a brick protruding and she clambered up. Only Brew grabbing hold of her prevented her from falling in."

Harriet shivered at the thought of what might have happened. But surely Becca was saying that Nancy was saved?

"He went straight to my father and begged him to cover the well, to make it safe. Before he was able to do so, Nancy sneaked back the next day. Perhaps she had another wish to make. We will never know. You can guess what happened. Our father blamed Brew for taking Nancy to the well. Brew blamed our father for not immediately making it safe. In my dreams I still hear them shouting at each other. After that day they barely spoke a word and, when he was eighteen, my brother ran away to join the army. We were reunited only last week."

"And were they reconciled, Major Ware and the squire?"

"No. My father wasn't present. Brew had written to him some weeks ago asking, as I understand from my mother, for a reconciliation. He chose not to reply. Our meeting was only brought about because Papa showed Mama the letter sometime after he had received it. She wrote to Brew and arranged for us to meet. And now I fear it is too late and that they will never speak again. Have you not wondered, Harriet, why Brew was not present at the Carstairs family's soirée when our families are so close? He was worried he would embarrass our friends if our father cut him in public. Better, he said, that he stayed away."

It was all much clearer now. Harriet realised that the major would always put others before himself. Had he not been extraordinarily kind to her when talking of John? She took Becca's now still hands in her own. "I don't begin to know what to say to you. I am honoured for your confidence and pray that speaking of your troubles will in some way help to ease your pain." But she was thinking of Brew and the anguish he had carried with him all these years. Of the blame he took upon himself for his sister's death. And inside she wept for him.

Shortly afterwards, the gentlemen joined them and confidences were for the time being at an end. Gil, the first to enter the room, wore a tight-fitting dark blue coat with ivory buttons over a cream embroidered waistcoat, which in colour exactly matched his silk breeches. His cravat was, for him, a modest cascade and served well for informal dining. Though his attire was less dazzling than his usual style, he was nonetheless turned out to perfection. As he bent his dark head low to speak to Amabel, Harriet could not help thinking what a handsome couple they made. She liked Gil and thought his confident good humour was just the thing for her quieter sister.

"What say we play charades?" he asked, his ready smile taking in the whole company. It was a game in which Amabel was found to excel and which everyone enjoyed, with the exception of Cornelius Ware, who chose to be an observer. No-one attempted to cajole him into it and that, in Harriet's opinion, told its own story. This man seemed to spend his life in a self-made prison. She resolved, if the opportunity should arise, to attempt to engage him in conversation. She would be prepared for a rebuff. For many rebuffs. But surely there must be a way to bring this man from the darkness into the light. Only time would tell.

CHAPTER NINE

By early afternoon Brew had inspected the whole of Austerly House, though he hesitated for a long time at the door of his old bedchamber before grasping the handle and entering. It was exactly as he remembered it. He was aware that his parents rarely welcomed visitors to their home, and certainly none were ever invited to stay. He suffered a moment of dejection, reflecting on how lonely his mother must have been. He realised now that she had thrown all her energy and love into caring for himself and Becca, and self-loathing was his uppermost emotion as he accepted the pain his departure must have caused her. What was it she had she said in her letter? *Please let it be that I no longer have to grieve for you.*

He walked over to the dresser upon which stood a jug and bowl. He smiled, recalling his early efforts at shaving himself. How proud he had been of that first facial hair. He moved around the room, touching this and that and remembering. The ache in his chest and the constriction in his throat both threatened to overwhelm him, and he made a hasty retreat. The only rooms he didn't enter were the bedchambers of his parents and Rebecca, out of respect for their privacy, and Nancy's room, which he knew would be an ordeal he was not ready to face.

"Well, it's taken you time enough to get down to the kitchen, I must say," complained the cook, Alice Gardner, with all the familiarity of an old retainer when Brew finally reached that part of the house. But there was no mistaking her moist eyes and trembling chin. She raised the corner of her pinafore to wipe away her tears before exclaiming, "You've been that long

I've had time to make some muffins, just as you used to like them. Mr Gardner has gone to fetch you some ale as, like me, he knew you would be down here sooner or later. Now, sit yourself down at my table, like when you was a lad, for I'll not let you out of my kitchen until you've something inside you."

She gave him another hug and a shed a few more tears before Brew did as he was bid, only to jump to his feet almost immediately when Jacob Gardner the gardener (it had always made him smile) entered the room. He shook his hand and clapped him on the shoulder, almost overbalancing. The old man caught him as he stumbled but made no remark. It seemed word had already gone through the house about the young master's injury.

"Now I know I'm home," Brew said to Mrs Gardner with a broad grin as he took a bite from a still warm muffin. "You've not lost your touch."

He remained for some time, talking of inconsequential things. They didn't question him, nor did he supply any information as to what he'd been doing all these years other than to say, "You'll be proud of me, I know, when I tell you I rose to the rank of major." He had as a child bent the ear of both, and it was Mr Gardner who had fashioned many a sword for him from the wood in the grounds.

Eventually the man bore him outside, talking all the while, telling him how hard he had tried to maintain the kitchen garden and that at the front of the house. The rest, however, was beyond him. "I did my best, sir," he finished.

"I'm sure you did, but it is too great a task for one man with scant help." Judging that if he could not trust this old retainer there was no hope for anyone, Brew said, "It will change, Jacob, if you will but hold on. No word to my father — you must promise me that — but it is my intention to put the place to rights. I have the means and the will."

"Well, I hope it may be in my lifetime, although the likelihood of that ain't great, sir, not as how you and the master aren't exactly convivial with each other."

Brew was aware of the truth of this statement but said positively that there were many changes to come and that he relied on him to help, so he'd just better take good care of himself until the time came. Back in the hall, emotionally if not physically exhausted, he told them all he would return the next day to inspect the stables and, more extensively, the grounds.

"Would you be wishful to see Mr Pullman, sir?" Kettersham asked.

"Not at the moment, William. It wouldn't be appropriate for me to talk with my father's steward without his knowledge, although there are some things I might need to discuss with him after I see how the land lies. That will be for another day. I must get back to The Bertie Arms before they give my room, and more importantly my dinner, to another guest."

As Brew sat down to his meal at the inn, the Lambert ladies were attending yet another party. The friendship that had begun so well between Harriet and Becca continued to flourish. Harriet told Rebecca about her previous visit to London and her betrothal to John Downing. She was fully conscious of the honour of being entrusted with the other's problems and felt compelled to reciprocate.

"Oh no, how awful for you," the younger woman said. "Have you never met anyone else for whom you might develop a tendre?"

Only one, thought Harriet, but she wasn't prepared to confide that piece of information to Brew's sister. In any case, it was early days and she was by no means sure she felt anything stronger than friendship. "No, for I was never in London again, and not long after John my father too passed away." She sighed deeply. "It was a bad time for us all, particularly for my mother. My father was not an old man and it was illness that took him from us, not age. I think it took Mama a long time to come to terms with her loss, unexpected as it was. And then the management of the estate somehow fell upon my shoulders."

Becca's eyes widened with respect, but Harriet just laughed.

"No, I am not an object of pity. I love my life and would have preferred to remain in Kent, but my mother wouldn't hear of it. So here I am thinking of all the tasks that will be waiting for me when I return home and absolutely longing to be out riding. It is my greatest hobby."

"Are you not then enjoying yourself?"

Again Harriet laughed. "Immensely. Far more than I had anticipated. What a creature I am to desire the best of both worlds. But what of you? What would you wish for?"

It was Rebecca's turn to smile, and then to frown, which led her companion to ask if anything was wrong.

"You will remember what I told you, about the day at the wishing well? I knew how things were at Austerly and I adored my father. He was a different man before the accident — you wouldn't recognise him. I don't myself. Anyway, it happened that he inherited an estate but not the means to maintain it. It has, in my opinion, been the ruin of him and then, after Nancy, he lost heart completely. He still tries, but I fear my home is a lost cause. How preferable it would have been had Papa been the incumbent of a curacy without the responsibilities that were forced upon him. It would have suited him so much better."

"But you were saying, on the day of the accident…?"

"Ah yes. Well, you must remember I was only five years old at the time." Becca took a deep breath, as though to confess something truly significant. "I wished I might marry a prince." Then she curled up laughing as the memory of the girl she was came back to her.

"Well, I don't suppose you'll find too many of those in London," Harriet said, joining in her mirth.

Becca became serious again. "My wish was for my father and for my brother. Had I married a prince, doubtless he would have been very rich and able to settle all Papa's debts, as well as buying Brew a commission and having the means for us all to live the rest of our lives in luxury. Things are always more simple when you're a child, aren't they? It seemed then to be a sensible answer to all our problems."

Harriet asked if it was still her wish, but Becca said she had long given up that dream. "But there is no doubt I must marry someone. The bequest from my godmother was sufficient only to fund our trip to London with a very small amount left over. I would, if I am able, relieve my father of the responsibility of maintaining me. But I must be honest with you: I worry that I will not take. I no longer look for riches, only to find someone with whom I can be comfortable. Who I am able to respect and look up to."

"But what of love?"

"My circumstances are such that I cannot be choosy. I believe my father's case to be desperate. The sooner I marry, the better it will be for him."

Harriet could only think what a sad situation it was. At least for her own part money was not an issue and she could, if she chose, live agreeably at Merivale House and want for nothing. It renewed her impatience with the perception that marriage was the only occupation for a young woman. Unsure what to say next, she was for once grateful for the approach of the gentleman in the gaudy striped waistcoat. "Becca, stand up now, please, and come with me," she said urgently.

Rebecca responded immediately and together they walked across the room to join their mothers, who were in conversation. When Harriet explained that this gentleman had been pursuing her to an unwelcome degree, Rebecca suggested that perhaps she might steal him away. "Might he not be the prince I have so long awaited?" she jested.

Louisa and Elizabeth looked up at their approach, and immediately demanded to join in the joke that was evidently causing both young ladies so much amusement. The gentleman was warded off, as was the continuation of a difficult discussion.

Brew was feeling considerably calmer when, after a hearty breakfast, he rode to Austerly the next morning. The worst hurdle had been cleared, and he was looking forward to visiting the stream where he had fished as a young man, the copse where he'd had sword fights with an imaginary adversary — or his sisters, when he'd been able to persuade them — and the stables he'd haunted as a child. Whistling to himself as he went, his thoughts ran over everything that had happened the previous day. There was no doubt that everyone had been delighted to see him. He was grateful for that because, as with his family, he had left without a word to any of them.

The whistling stopped, for it was something one only did when happy, and it was all at once brought home to him how cruel he had been to his mother. An eighteen-year-old youth, he had thought himself a man. He'd believed it was acceptable to turn his back on everything and go. Well, he hadn't been a man, not then, though the army had definitely made one of him. His mother, if not his father, had deserved more. Oh, he'd left a note for her, short and to the point: *My father does not want me here. I'm going to enlist.* His older self eventually realised how cruel this had been.

Brew wondered how his mother and sister were faring in London. He gave little thought to the squire, trying to push away the dismissal he'd received in St James's Street. His mood lifted as he thought of Becca and wondered if she was as yet any closer to finding her prince, and a smile hovered about his lips. He would somehow arrange to visit them as soon as he returned to the city, and this he resolved to do the next day. He was eager to see them again and to try to capture something of what he had lost over so many years.

Stopping at the house before exploring the estate, he was delighted to find that Mrs Gardner had prepared and packed some food for him, mindful that he would probably be out the whole day.

"You are a treasure. In fact, I shall take a rod with me and try my hand again at fishing. Something to eat will, I'm sure, be very welcome."

Mr Gardner put his wife's offering into the saddlebag and went off to fetch a rod for the young master, as he still insisted on calling him. Pru and Kettersham stood on the steps and waved him off. With his horse at a walking pace to begin with, Brew was able to see that things were in just as sad a case as he had imagined. Dilapidation was everywhere. He could not be dispirited for long, though, venturing across this land that only now did he realise he loved. One day it would be his, but he would give much to be able to rectify so many years of negligence more speedily. As things stood with his father, he knew this was at present out of the question. Not one to be pulled down by things beyond his control, he decided to put it out of his mind, trusting that a solution would occur to him when he was least trying to find it. For now he would give himself up to the pleasure of a still, sunny day.

After inspecting broken fences and fallen shacks, he made his way to the stream. Here he sat down to enjoy his repast and, after spending a while in fruitless angling, he lay on his back with his hands behind his head and looked up at the sky, unbroken by any cloud. He found himself thinking of Harriet Lambert, picturing her chestnut hair and frank green eyes. And, with a smile, he dozed off in the sunshine.

Brew awoke a while later feeling chilled. The afternoon now was considerably advanced and he jumped to his feet, cursing as he almost fell by reason of his unstable leg. He gathered together the remnants of his feast and, together with his rod, took them to where he had left his horse tied to a low branch and grazing happily. He led him to the water to drink before mounting and riding back to the house. Here he was detained for a fair spell, because there was no way he was going to risk offending these people who had been so kind to him. There were tears as he left, for no-one, least of all himself, knew when he would be able to return.

Fortunately, though it was now dark, the sky was still clear and the sun had been replaced by a near full moon. He made a good meal when he got back to The Bertie Arms and gave instructions to François to be ready to leave immediately after breakfast the next morning.

The journey back to London was far less tedious. He had a lot to think about, and the first thing would be to find a way of seeing his mother and sister without his father's knowledge. He had also come to the realisation that he wished very much to renew his acquaintance with Miss Harriet Lambert.

CHAPTER TEN

In London there were three young ladies who, had they been so inclined, could have congratulated themselves on their success. The company of the two Misses Lambert and Miss Ware was sought wherever they went, whether they be walking in the park, attending a soirée, or riding in the carriage that Lady Sawcroft kept in town and insisted on putting at their disposal.

Louisa Lambert was enjoying herself tremendously, her arrangements for Amabel's ball being well under way. It was to take place in four weeks' time to coincide with the next full moon, and invitations had already been written and sent. There was much to be done, not the least of which was to order her younger daughter's ball gown and one for herself and Harriet. Louisa had a great flair for organisation and rose to meet every task. She was ably aided by both her girls, Amabel having the neatest handwriting and addressing the invitations and Harriet discussing with her such matters as the number of candles required.

"And how many extra maids shall we engage, Mama?" she asked. "Oh, and I have noted down some dishes which I think we might serve for supper."

"I see you have brought your managing skills with you to London from Merivale. You have always been at your most happy when there is a job to be tackled," Louisa observed.

Harriet laughed. "I can hardly believe how much there is to do! And last time I barely did a thing to help you. You are amazing," she said, giving her mother a hug.

Louisa laughed also but said only that she enjoyed it very much and didn't look upon it as a chore. Between them, and with the aid of a less experienced but nonetheless equally enthusiastic Amabel, the ladies made light work of what might otherwise have been an exhausting task.

"Do you recall, Mama, the musicians you hired for my own ball?" asked Harriet. "They were excellent, in my opinion."

"I do, Harriet, and I have already contacted them to see if they are free on that day. Happily I have had a reply in the affirmative and have engaged them."

"Had you thought of adding more mirrors to those already in place?"

"I don't think it necessary. You will recall the room was sufficiently well-lit the last time, and we have increased the number of candles. I believe it would appear too contrived. It may not be every day that we give a ball, but I'd like to think the setting will look natural. Spectacular but natural."

"Yes, Mama, but then anything you undertake would be spectacular."

"Speaking of which, do please see where Amabel has got to. It will shortly be time for us to go for her next fitting."

Harriet went obediently, and an hour later the younger Miss Lambert was standing in the dressmaker's back room. It was a simple gown, exactly right for a young woman of eighteen years appearing at a ball to be held in her honour, and it was entirely ivory. A satin slip under an over-dress of gauze, its only embellishments were satin ribbon around the edges of the sleeves and beneath the bodice, this one tied in a tiny bow. The theme continued at the hem, where the seamstress had fashioned a wide border by adding five layers of ribbon at the bottom. Amabel looked delicate and almost ethereal, something upon which the dressmaker commented, making all three ladies smile. Amabel stroked her fingers along the ribbon, drawing a reproof from her mother.

"You will not look heavenly if your gown is adorned with smudges. Do keep your hands down, dearest."

"Yes, Mama," Amabel answered demurely but with such a gleam in her eyes as to make everyone laugh, even the poor woman who was trying to fit the dress to her slender form.

Louisa and Harriet were next to be fitted, and the day was by then too far advanced for them to indulge in any more shopping. They returned to Hay Hill, exhausted but happy and, for once, spent a quiet evening at home. Replies to the invitations were coming in all the time, but there was one that Harriet looked for which had not yet arrived. Major Ware was back in town, she knew, for she'd had the information from Rebecca while walking with her in the park.

"He has sent a note to Mama, and we are trying to contrive a way of seeing him without Papa's knowledge. It is hateful to adopt such deception, but unless my father relents we have no choice."

"Would it help if I explained to my mother? Not the circumstances, of course, but I'm sure she would be happy to accommodate you if that would help resolve the problem."

"That would be most kind. You won't object if first I ask mine? She is aware that I have confided in you, but it may be that…" She stopped, seemingly unsure how to go on, but Harriet understood perfectly and said she would wait to hear.

Next time Harriet saw Brew was in Hay Hill, for her offer had been accepted. Louisa had placed a small withdrawing room at the disposal of the Wares, and she and her daughters waited there with Elizabeth and Rebecca for the arrival of the major. Refreshments were served before they removed themselves and Harriet had the opportunity of a few quiet words with Brew while the rest were engaged in conversation.

"Forgive me, Major, but my mother has not yet received a reply from you to her invitation to my sister's ball. I do hope you will be able to join us."

"It is for me to apologise, but perhaps you will understand better when I explain my apparent rudeness. I know from Rebecca that you are aware of our family's situation. Indeed, it is very generous of Mrs Lambert to accommodate us in this way."

"Yes, your sister was kind enough to take me into her confidence. It is my understanding that you have not spoken to your father for many years."

"That is true. What perhaps you do not know is that he gave me the cut direct when I ran into him unexpectedly two weeks ago, and now I am at a loss as to know how to proceed. You see, I am aware that he and my mother, and my sister too, have also received an invitation. Imagine how it would be if he were to do the same again. It could not go unnoticed, and I would be reluctant to put any of you in such a position. You know how ready people are to gossip. That sort of thing would taint the evening for you all and that is why I haven't as yet responded, for I cannot at present think of a way around the problem. You may be certain that it is my dearest wish to come."

This he said with a warmth she could not mistake. The major wasn't a man to utter empty compliments. Harriet was more disappointed than she liked to admit at the possibility that he might not be at Hay Hill on such an important occasion.

"Is there no chance of a reconciliation?"

Brew looked into her eyes. "I have tried. Did my sister tell you that I wrote to him? That he didn't even acknowledge my letter? And then went to the extent of crossing the road to avoid me? Sadly I think we are far from a resolution."

"But whether it's at Amabel's ball or some other function, surely it is inevitable that you should meet eventually."

"Almost certainly, but I would not have that happen in your home or cause you any avertible distress."

Harriet rose as she saw her mother and sister do the same. "We will leave you now. I hope you might be able to find a way through this predicament. I believe Mama has asked you to remain for tea and directed the staff to say that we are not at home to visitors, should anyone else call. I look forward to seeing you later."

Brew watched Harriet leave the room in her mother's wake and turned to embrace his own before addressing his sister.

"Any sign of that prince yet, Becca?"

It lightened the mood a little, as had been his intention. This was going to be a difficult and emotional meeting, and he wanted to make it as easy as possible for all of them.

"No, how could there be indeed, when there is none to outshine my handsome brother?"

"Princes are everywhere, are they not, Becca?" Brew went on. "Brothers are a rarer breed."

He then became grave again and suggested they sit down and see if they could not find a way forward. An hour later, they were no closer to an answer, having abandoned the seemingly impossible task within a few minutes and moved on to other things. Elizabeth asked him how he had found things at Austerly.

"You may imagine my anxiety, but I need not have worried. I was welcomed with open arms, literally, by William and Pru, and later by the Gardners. It seems they still hold me in some affection. I cannot imagine why, when I remember all the times that I ran rings around them as a child. Would you believe, Mama, I had been in the house barely above an hour or two when Mrs Gardner presented me with some freshly baked muffins? Then poor old Jacob insisted on showing me the garden, and I could tell how distressed he was at the state things were in. I know you will forgive me when I tell you that I made them aware of my ambition to bring the estate back to bygone days. It seemed to give them all some hope."

"You will make a good master when the time comes, Brew. In the meantime, I wish there was some way we could bring your father round. I am no longer able to reach him. We are as strangers living in the same house," Elizabeth said. Her eyes misted over and Brew and Becca both rose to comfort her.

"The Carstairs family are such old acquaintances, Mama. How do you think it would be if I paid a visit when I know you are to be there? Surely my father could not be so rude as to make a scene in their home. Nor could he storm out of the house, not if you were there too, for it would be unthinkable that he should leave without you."

He watched as hope spread over Elizabeth's face. "We could take Sarah and Matthew into our confidence. I do not hesitate to tell you that they have been very good to me. I don't know how I deserve such friends, but so it is. Yes, it is possible. But are you prepared, Brew, to suffer the humiliation of another rejection?"

"I would do anything to be able to come and go as I please. He cannot, I believe, prevent me from coming to see you and Becca at Austerly, but he could make it very uncomfortable for me to do so and, worse, for you too. He must be made to see that he is tearing our family apart. And if he doesn't, well, I shall come and see you anyway. I would prefer it, though, if I could come in peace."

His sister broke in. "Would you tell him of your current circumstances and your desire to make reparations?"

"If he will allow me to do so, then yes. I just hope he doesn't let his pride stand in his way."

Elizabeth promised to talk to Sarah as soon as possible and let Brew know when it might be convenient for him to call. "And maybe then you might be able to come to the Lamberts' ball. They too have been exceedingly kind to us."

"And Harriet has become almost like a sister to me," Becca said, before bursting into tears at the memory of her own real sister.

Once Brew, Rebecca and Elizabeth had finished their discussion and had been escorted to where the Lambert ladies were waiting for them, Louisa asked the footman to order tea and they all sat down to talk. She was determined they would speak only of inconsequential things, because she knew the last hour or so must have been a trial for them all, but it was Brew who raised the subject of the forthcoming ball.

"I must apologise for not having responded to your invitation, Mrs Lambert. I am honoured and would very much like to accept." She was about to reply, but he held up his hand. "Unfortunately, circumstances are such that I must ask for a little more time before I can give you a definite answer. I would be happy to stand down if my procrastination is causing problems for you but, if you can wait, I am sure I will be able to give you a reply within two to three days." He looked questioningly at his mother and received a reassuring look.

"You would be most welcome, Major Ware, even were you only to make an appearance on the day itself," Louisa assured him.

"I hope my manners are not that bad!"

They were laughing as tea arrived, and they talked generally for a short while before Elizabeth stood up, anxious now to contact her friend as speedily as possible and to put their plan into motion. Brew remained a few moments longer, asking Harriet if she could spare a minute or two. Left alone in the room, he turned his charming smile upon her and asked if she might be willing to risk another carriage outing, if he could prevail upon Gil and Amabel to join them again.

"As long as you can promise he will not this time conjure up visions of ghostly highwaymen, I am certain my sister will be as delighted as myself. Would it be outrageous of me to ask you to take us to Richmond Park? Amabel has heard me talk of it and expressed a desire to see it for herself and, if I'm honest, I would dearly love to go there again."

"And this time we shall bring our own picnic. For now I shall bid you farewell, but I hope it will not be long before you hear from me. Let us hope the weather is again kind. Certainly the few weeks since our last outing have made a difference, and it is considerably warmer than when last we went."

As he spoke he took her hand and, raising it to his lips, kissed her fingers. Harriet was at once surprised and more than a little flustered. It was no longer customary for a gentleman to salute a lady in this way, and she felt heat rising up her neck. Brew did not see, for he had left the room as he spoke, but Harriet could feel herself tingling long after he had gone.

CHAPTER ELEVEN

The major's meeting with his father had been a mixed blessing. Armed with the knowledge that his family would be taking tea with the Carstairs family, Brew had arranged his visit to coincide with theirs, taking Gil with him in case he was tempted to abandon his quest. It was something he was looking forward to with considerable apprehension but, he told himself, somebody had to make the first move and it obviously wasn't going to be his parent.

The two younger men entered the drawing room unannounced. It was, after all, Gil's family's town house. Five pairs of eyes looked at Brew with differing expressions. Sarah and Matthew Carstairs were welcoming as ever. Elizabeth and Becca looked decidedly uneasy and, on the squire's face, was an expression his son was hard put to read. Anger? Certainly he was flexing his fingers on the arms of his chair. Anguish? The muscles in his neck stood out like cords. At least he didn't jump up and storm out of the room.

Brew moved to his hosts and greeted them as the old friends they were. He would never forget the kindness they had shown him when as a boy he had haunted their home. He embraced his mother, kissed his sister on the cheek and turned at last to face his father.

"I hope I find you well, sir," he began. "I would be most obliged if you would, with Mrs Carstairs' permission, grant me a few minutes alone with you. There are things I think we should discuss."

The squire's decision hung in the balance. Brew could tell that from his laboured breathing and the sweat that broke out on his face. Finally, after what seemed an age, the older man spoke and Brew could at last let go of his breath.

"Of course. Sarah," he said, turning to his hostess, "would you excuse us for a while?"

"Certainly. The library is free. You know your way."

Cornelius rose and his son moved aside to allow him to pass before him. He was grateful for the aid of his stick, for his legs no longer felt as if they belonged to him. The squire preceded him into the library and sat down behind a desk, indicating to his son a chair on the other side. The physical barrier between them was no greater, Brew felt, than the tension that separated them. Surprisingly, his father's first words were regarding his injury.

"You sustained that abroad, I imagine. Does it pain you much?"

"No, sir. I hardly notice it these days. Occasionally it lets me down, which is why I use the walking aid."

There was a silence which seemed to lengthen until Brew feared it would be difficult to break, so he said, for the sake of any utterance, "And you, sir? You are well, I hope."

Cornelius ignored the question, remarking instead, "You are grown from boy to man. Did army life live up to your expectations?"

"Yes, sir, and more. I was fortunate to be spotted by a superior officer who enabled me to progress through the ranks. With his sponsorship I attained my majority."

"I am aware I was unable to purchase a commission for you," Cornelius said. The bitterness he felt was evident in the clipped tone he adopted. "But then, I wasn't given the opportunity to try, was I? You just disappeared. That is what I find hardest to forgive. You broke your mother's heart."

Suddenly the conversation had turned and it was Brew who was on the defensive. He accepted the remonstrance. It was true, after all. "I am older and I hope wiser now. And she has forgiven me."

"I am aware from the touching scene I witnessed earlier that you have already seen each other since your return. Why then would you wish to speak to me?"

"Are you not also my family? For the sake of Mama, and of Becca, can we not arrive at some semblance of civility?"

"Nancy was also family." Cornelius spoke the words quietly, almost as if they were forced from him.

To Brew, it was far harsher than had he shouted. Tearing at his hair, he walked to the window and stared out, though he saw nothing but his sister's tiny body. He began to sob silently, releasing something he had held within for so many years. As if through a mist, he heard his father's voice.

"Enough! That remark was uncalled for and I apologise." Brew had never heard his father apologise for anything before. "We cannot go back. Nothing will return Nancy to us and nothing, I fear, will mend the breach between us. For your mother's sake we will in public put on a united front. I can offer no more."

It was more than Brew had hoped for. He decided now was not the time to make his sire aware of his change in fortune. In such a precarious situation, he did not wish to risk upsetting the applecart. So all he said was, "You will not turn away from me again, should we meet?"

"That was a mistake. I shall not do it again."

There was nothing more to be said, for the time being at any rate. They returned to the others and Gil had the good sense to bear his friend off.

"Is this another of those times we get drunk, old boy?"

"An excellent idea, Gil, but it could have been worse. We are at least communicating now."

"Then let us go and drink to the success of your mission. To tell you the truth, I didn't think you stood much chance of bringing him round."

"To tell you the truth, neither did I." The tension eased, and they headed for St James's.

Two days after the Ware family had visited Hay Hill, Louisa received a reply from Major Ware thanking her for her kind invitation to Miss Amabel Lambert's ball and saying he would be delighted to attend. Harriet, although she was pleased, was on tenterhooks, anxious to know what had transpired. She wondered whether Brew would explain when they drove out to Richmond Park together.

However, when the day of the projected outing arrived, he made no mention of the circumstances. When Harriet said how glad she was that he would be able to join them, he merely replied that he too was glad and looked forward immensely to the evening, when he hoped she might sit out one or two of the dances to converse with him, aware as she was that he was unable to participate. He said this without any sign of self-consciousness, apparently satisfied that she had accepted him for what he was.

"Spring seems to have arrived early this year," Harriet said to Brew as they made their way to the park. She was seated beside him in the carriage, with Amabel and Mr Carstairs behind. "We couldn't have chosen a finer day. I am certain you will be pleased that I managed to persuade Mama not to send an extra picnic basket 'just in case'. I had a hard time stopping her, I can tell you."

Brew laughed aloud. "Mothers are all the same, are they not? At least, mine certainly was when I was a child. She has had no opportunity in recent years to compel me to eat anything I don't like, but you wouldn't credit the number of things I stuffed in my pockets when my hands were hidden from the table. She used to insist that we had one meal together each day, my parents, my sisters and I. Poor Nurse grumbled away each time but she never told Mama, not that I ever heard about anyway."

Harriet said nothing but reflected that his life had obviously been a normal and happy one before the tragic accident that Becca had told her about. She found the knowledge comforting.

"Like your sister, I have never before visited Richmond Park, Miss Lambert. I must say that I am looking forward to it immensely. Gil tells me we owe a debt of gratitude to one John Lewis, a brewer who secured public rights of access some sixty years ago."

"How very interesting. There must be a huge amount of history surrounding such a vast area, particularly with its royal connections."

The road was quiet enough now and, proceeding at a trot for the time being, Brew was able to withdraw his concentration from his driving to look at Harriet.

"Are you warm enough?" he asked. "Nice as the day is, there is still a breeze and I wouldn't want you to catch a chill."

Harriet was touched by his concern and answered that she was sufficiently cosy. She was wearing a pelisse and with the blanket Brew had laid over her knees, she defied anyone to be cold. It was an open carriage and she glanced over her shoulder to observe her sister and Mr Carstairs sitting in agreeable silence behind her. Amabel's hands were tucked inside her muff, but Harriet felt sure she was deriving just as much warmth from the proximity of her companion. She was herself quite content to sit in the silence into which she and the major had lapsed.

While for the most part paying attention to the surrounding countryside, Harriet surreptitiously studied his profile. It was a rugged face; she suspected it had partly been made so by his time in the army and the many hours he must have spent outside in all weathers. An aquiline nose added a degree of severity but this was softened by blondish hair, a shade darker than his sister's, she noted, some of which escaped from beneath the rim of his hat. He turned to look at her, as if aware of her examination, and his features broke into a smile that banished any hardness she might have imagined and at the same time caused her stomach to lurch. It was a sensation she recognised but had not felt for a very long time.

"Are you worried I will turn us over, Miss Lambert?"

"Not at all," she said, recovering her composure. "You have a light touch and have your horses well in hand."

"Are you then an admirer of the sport?"

"Not merely an admirer but a participant also. At least, I am when at home. My father taught me from a very young age and he was himself a renowned whip. It is what I most miss when I am in London."

"But this is lamentable. Surely it is something that can be rectified."

"It could, of course, but I deemed it foolish to do so, knowing as I did how much time would be spent shopping with Mama and my sister, and making arrangements for Amabel's ball. I miss riding even more than driving, but I know I leave Rhapsody in good hands."

Brew had given his attention back to the road but at this he glanced at her again, the expression on his face telling her that he thought he beheld a rare creature indeed. She laughed, something she did often when spending time with this man.

"Is it so extraordinary then?"

"Let us say it is unexpected."

Little more was said, and it was some considerable time later that he swung his team through the Robin Hood Gate and into the park.

Leaving Walter to take care of the horses and carriage, the party found a sheltered place beneath some trees and sank down with all the ease of a group of people who were comfortable in each other's company.

"I sincerely trust that you have stocked this basket with delicious fare, for I must tell you after that delightful drive I am absolutely ravenous," Amabel declared. Any diffidence she may once have felt at being in such close proximity to two young gentlemen had been left behind.

"That particular task was assigned to Mr Carstairs, Miss Lambert, so it is with him you must take issue if all is not to your satisfaction."

It seemed unlikely that anything Mr Carstairs did would fail to come up to Miss Lambert's expectations and she declared, once the meal was over, that she had eaten her fill and could now concentrate on the beautiful surroundings.

"Are you content to watch from here, or would you prefer to go for a walk?" Brew asked the ladies.

"A walk would be desirable after sitting for so long, don't you think, Amabel?"

"Oh yes, Harriet, for there is so much to see. Far more, I think, than we could ever hope to absorb in one visit."

"I am more than happy to escort you ladies again, if that is your wish."

Their laughter mingled, but Harriet said, "I'm sure my sister did not mean to coerce you into another outing, sir."

"I can assure you, Miss Lambert, that coercion is entirely unnecessary. What do you think, Gil? Shall we go in that direction?" Brew asked, pointing to where a number of riders were taking some exercise.

With Harriet on his arm, Brew realised that she was containing her excitement and moderating her pace in consideration of his injury. He was quite touched and assured her that speed was no problem, but rather that he used his stick for stability. "Just in case I stumble, though I'm glad to say that it happens rarely these days."

She was for a moment filled with consternation. "I'm so sorry. I had no intention of bringing my anxiety to your attention. Only that you should be easy. Please forgive me."

He smiled again. "There is nothing to forgive. If I had not been aware of your eagerness to cover the ground, I'd never have noticed. And here we are. One or two beautiful animals, are there not?" he said as they observed the riders from alongside a broad drive that had been cut through the trees. "And even had you not confided in me earlier, I would by now have discovered your passion. It shines out of your eyes." Brew became serious once more. "There must be some way we can arrange for you to go riding in London, even if you can't bring your horse — Rhapsody, was it? — to town."

Harriet quite liked the way he said 'we can arrange'. She had been so much in the habit of organising things, both at Merivale and to some extent at Hay Hill, that she found it refreshing to think someone else might take the reins, as it were. She had no doubt, knowing what she did of the major, that he would make it happen.

"Are they not deer?" Amabel squealed from behind them, pointing off into the distance. "I think they are, but I cannot see well enough through the trees and the sun is in my eyes."

"They are quite far away, but I feel sure you are right," Gil replied, raising his own hands to shield his eyes. "I wonder if they are hunted here."

"I imagine so, old boy, but whether or not one would require a permit I am not sure. I suspect it would be the case."

It was left to Harriet to point out, "I would not wish to be the one to put a damper on things, but Amabel's remark about the sun has reminded me that we have a long journey home. Perhaps it is time we returned to the carriage, loth though I am to leave this beautiful place. We need to consider how long it will take, and I wouldn't want Mama to grow concerned if we arrive home after dark."

"In that case, Miss Lambert, we must definitely arrange to do it again — perhaps a little later in the season, when the days are drawing out and we can spend a longer time admiring our surroundings," said Brew as they prepared to depart.

The following day, Harriet was walking with Rebecca in Hyde Park, their mothers just ahead of them.

"My brother came to see us this morning," said Rebecca. "He told me you had experienced a delightful day in Richmond yesterday."

"It was outstanding, Becca, and vast. Far bigger than where we are now," Harriet said, indicating their surroundings. She waited, but when Rebecca said nothing, she blurted out the question that had been on her mind for days. "And the major's visit to the Carstairs? Did that go well?"

"Brew didn't tell you? No, I suppose he wouldn't have. I can tell you that Mama gripped my hand so tightly when he came in that I nearly shrieked. I was no less nervous than she, but I have to say my brother carried it off far more successfully than any of us would have deemed possible."

"Are they reconciled then, he and your father?"

The drawing together of her friend's eyebrows indicated this was not the case. "From what he told me of their discussion, I fear there will never be a full reconciliation, but Papa has agreed at least to acknowledge Brew in public and to behave with dignity. I think that's the best we can hope for, for the time being. Maybe, if they see each other often enough, things will improve. In the meantime, I can only be grateful that there is no risk of an inappropriate altercation and that Brew may visit us in Duke Street, even if my father does choose to absent himself from my mother's drawing room."

"It must be a relief to you all."

"Certainly it means the world to Mama. Her reunion with Brew was obviously emotional, but she seems to have a much more relaxed attitude now, about everything. And I am able to go to parties in the knowledge that on many occasions my big brother will be there. Such a treat I did not expect when first we came to London."

"You are enjoying yourself?"

"People have been so kind, your own mother being one of them. I know there is no ball being held in my honour, but I care not for that. Everything else a young woman experiences in her debut season is within my reach so yes, I am enjoying every moment."

The two older women drew to a halt, as did Harriet and Rebecca behind them.

"Here is Aunt Matilda, come to restore Amabel to us," Louisa said as the old lady's carriage drew up beside them.

Lady Sawcroft muttered to them but pinched her niece's arm playfully. "You may have her back, Louisa, for I do not know if I am coming or going, so many times has my coachman been obliged to draw to a halt as some buck or other wished to pay his respects. I will say this for you, young lady," she said, addressing Amabel, "you have very pretty manners and you are a credit to your mother. I look forward to seeing how you conduct yourself at your ball, but I have no fears that you will disgrace your family. None at all. Now, be off with you so that I may go home, for I am quite exhausted." With this parting shot, she leaned back against the squabs and was driven away.

"Exhausted indeed, Mama. I swear my aunt has more energy than someone half her age," said Amabel.

"Of course she does, but never say so in her hearing, for she is forever telling everyone how fragile she is."

"She terrifies me," Rebecca said with a bemused smile.

"There is no need, my dear. My sister-in-law's bark is considerably worse than her bite."

The ladies proceeded, all amused by this larger than life character, but they found her words to be true as they too had cause to pause many times to exchange greetings with Amabel's admirers, and with Rebecca's and Harriet's also. This included the gentleman with the striped waistcoat, whose attentions had become very pronounced. Very pronounced indeed.

CHAPTER TWELVE

Recalling — after a nudge from Mr Carstairs — his promise to take his sister to the theatre, Major Ware was fortunate to find an evening when his mother, his sister and the Lambert ladies were all free. With Gil to act as an additional host, they were escorted in two carriages to Drury Lane.

For all three young women it was an exhilarating experience, neither Amabel nor Rebecca having been before and Harriet only once on her previous trip to town. They observed the show with rapt attention, and it wasn't until the interval that they had an opportunity to briefly take in their surroundings. Visitors entered the box and Major Ware and Gil Carstairs, the latter exceedingly reluctantly, moved back to make room for them. A well-dressed man of some thirty years engaged Miss Ware and the younger Miss Lambert in conversation, though to any observer it was evident that Rebecca was the object of his gallantry. Gil relaxed a little. Brew leaned back in the corner of the box, a smile of unholy amusement playing about his lips for, attendant upon Harriet, was Mr Chigwell, he of the predilection for striped waistcoats. She looked like nothing so much as a cornered rabbit and flung such a look of entreaty at him that he strolled again to the front to relieve her of a situation she was so evidently not enjoying.

"Miss Lambert, I trust I do not intrude, but I fear we must bid our friends adieu for the time being. I believe the next act is about to begin. How kind of you to have graced us with your company, Mr Chigwell. Good evening, sir."

The poor man had no choice but to leave, though not before Harriet had had a chance as they stood side by side to observe the difference in the two gentlemen's attire. Each made a statement but Major Ware, in his habitual black and silver, declared himself to be a man of taste and refinement.

The gentleman who had been talking to Amabel and Becca turned to Brew and introduced himself. "Dorian Fletcher at your service, sir. I hope I may meet you in Duke Street when I call to visit your sister. It is permitted?"

"Nothing to do with me, Mr Fletcher. I don't live there myself, but no doubt my mother will receive you."

He watched the rather exaggerated way the man bent over his sister's hand. Some instinct told him he was one to watch. A little too smooth, in Brew's opinion. And then Harriet was reprimanding him.

"How could you?" she said, barely controlling her irritation. "That man is annoying in the extreme."

"Dorian Fletcher? I didn't know you were acquainted with him."

"Don't pretend to misunderstand me, Major. You are very well aware that I am referring to Mr Chigwell."

"But he is obviously intent on charming himself into your favour. It would be cruel indeed were I to hinder him when he has an opportunity. No, don't berate me again. We must be quiet. The curtain is rising."

He seated himself beside her and almost laughed aloud. Harriet was biting her lip, but not with anger. She had, as did he, a fine appreciation for a joke. He was certain she would, if she could, wreak her revenge upon him later. He looked forward to it.

Curiosity took the major to Duke Street the next afternoon, and his luck was in. Dorian Fletcher was paying court to his sister, and it appeared that his compliments were welcome. It was hardly surprising. The man dressed well enough, unlike the court card who was so determinedly pursuing Miss Lambert. Adorning a pair of fine legs were cream pantaloons, and his dove-grey coat was worn over an ivory waistcoat. Well turned out and unobtrusive, and yet… Brew couldn't decide why he had misgivings. He mentioned it later to Gil, when both were for once dining at home in Grosvenor Square.

"A bit of an adventurer by all accounts. The *on dit* is that he's on the lookout for an heiress."

"He'll do himself no good hanging around my sister, then. Surely he must know Rebecca has no such expectations."

"You'd think so, wouldn't you? Allow me to top up your glass. A very nice claret, Brew, I must say. I have noticed that he's becoming a little particular in his attentions, though. It wouldn't be hard to fall in love with your sister, you know. She's a very beautiful young woman."

"What's this, Gil? I had thought your affections were engaged elsewhere."

"You know very well they are. Just remarking. She's a friend of mine, after all. Known her since she was a toddler. Best steer her away from Fletcher, though. The man doesn't have a feather to fly with and after all she's been through, well, I'd like to see her do better."

Brew raised an eyebrow but made no comment.

"Well, we all know how hard it's been for the squire. It would be nice to see Becca comfortably established, that's all I'm saying."

His host put his elbows on the table and rested his chin on his hands. "You think I should be watchful."

"That's it, Brew. Keep an eye on her."

So busy were the Lambert ladies that the days seemed to fly by, and before they could credit it the morning of Amabel's ball had arrived.

"I am so excited I don't know how to contain myself, Mama. And we are fortunate, are we not, that the weather is set fair. You and Harriet have worked so hard, I only pray I shall not disappoint either one of you."

"As if you could, dearest," her sister said, taking her hand and looking into her deep blue eyes. "You have in these past few weeks proved to be so well able to conduct yourself in public that you may have no qualms about committing a faux pas."

"No qualms, Harry! I am terrified."

"But why?" Louisa asked. "It is by no means your first appearance, after all."

Amabel looked from one to the other and took a deep breath. "Everyone will be looking at me. I have before now been able to sit a little aside without drawing attention to myself. But tonight…"

Louisa could find no fault with her daughter's modesty and, being of a practical nature, she judged it was time to distract her. "There is little you can do here, Amabel. Everything is underway and in good hands. I suggest you summon your abigail, walk down the hill and stroll once or twice around Berkeley Square. It will give you something else to think about and hopefully rid you of your fidgets."

"But can Harriet not come with me, Mama?"

"No, for it is she who has designed the layout of the garden. If, as I hope, the evening remains mild, some of our guests may well wish to take the air. Harriet has a nice touch, so I prefer she remain here to supervise."

"But is there nothing I can do?"

"Since I am rather fond of some of the glassware we have brought with us to town from Merivale, not to mention my favourite ornaments, I think it best we don't risk anything slipping through your fingers. Go now and by the time you return, you may have a while to relax before it is time to dress your hair."

Amabel went off muttering something about not being clumsy and if they thought she could relax, they might think again.

"Poor Amabel. I think you are right to attempt to give her thoughts another direction, Mama," said Harriet. "I'm not sure how successful your ruse will be, but at least it will keep her occupied. Now, if you will excuse me, I shall do as you suggested and inspect progress in the garden."

She spent a while outside making minor adjustments to her plans. Certainly she had a flair for decoration, and lanterns were hung in the trees and cushions placed on the stone benches. The garden was sufficiently large as to be divided into three sections and to each she added adornments of a different colour, making it seem almost as if they were separate rooms. Satisfied that her instructions were being adhered to, she went back inside to see if there was anything she might do to help her mother. She was surprised to find her entertaining Mr Chigwell, though she must have wished him elsewhere.

It became apparent that the gentleman had learned by some means or other of the forthcoming ball and had called to give his best wishes to Miss Amabel Lambert on her official coming out. That, at least, was what he said. However, his presence not having been requested for the evening, neither Louisa nor Harriet was fooled for a moment, there being no doubt in either of their minds that he was angling for an invitation. By nature a gregarious woman, Mrs Lambert was hard put not to fulfil the request that was so blatantly being put forth. It was, as balls went, to be quite an intimate affair and, knowing how distasteful his attentions were to her daughter, she managed to hold her tongue.

Harriet sat down and in her usual calm way merely said, "How kind of you to call, sir. I will of course pass on your kind wishes. You must know that the party is to be made up of only family and our closest friends. There are many whom we would have chosen to invite, but my sister is apprehensive of being overwhelmed, so the decision was made to ask only those with whom she is already acquainted. I hope we may have the pleasure of seeing you again soon at some other function." She then rose from her chair, leaving Mr Chigwell with no option but to do the same.

"Yes, well, I hope to see you very soon, Miss Lambert. Good day to you. And to you, Mrs Lambert."

The ladies managed to contain their mirth until he had left the room, but then Harriet broke into a peal of laughter and Louisa, similarly overcome, was left gasping for air. "Oh, well done, my dear! What a very tenacious young man. Do not on any account accept an offer from him, for I fear I couldn't maintain even an appearance of civility were I called upon to spend long in his company."

"I can promise you, Mama, that I had rather remain single than be married to such a pompous man. In any case, I should be subject to the headache were I to gaze upon the splendour of his wardrobe for too long. He reminds me of nothing so much as a callow youth experimenting with this and that until such time as he might find a suitable style. Understandable for a much younger man but he must be fast approaching thirty, if he hasn't attained that age already. No, you need have no fear in that direction."

All three ladies were gowned and ready in good time. Amabel wore her mother's pearls, the perfect accessory for her simple gown. Louisa, on being asked if she was happy with the result, remarked that she was delighted with the ivory-coloured silk gloves which had been bought for a song in that delightful bazaar.

Her daughter giggled. "And my slippers, Mama. Don't forget those, purchased at the same time and just when we were despairing of finding the right thing. They are so comfortable I feel I shall be able to dance all night."

"As well, since it is what will be expected of you. Now, where is your sister?"

At that moment Harriet walked into the room and her mother's breath caught in her throat, though she was at pains not to let her see. She was dressed in a gown of shimmering pale green silk, the bodice cut low with a band beneath it. The material flowed to the floor, seeming to have a life of its own. With short puff sleeves which tightened above the elbow, Harriet wore no jewellery save for a single pearl hung from a ribbon of the same colour. Her glorious chestnut hair was arranged in curls, a few of which had been allowed to drop to her shoulders, seemingly by accident but in fact arranged with great care by her maid to do exactly that. Into her curls was pinned a comb fashioned from tiny green rosebuds. She looked like what she was. Not a girl in her first season but a young lady, quietly assured and with a charm quite different from that of her sister. While Amabel was a captivatingly pretty English rose, Harriet was a very beautiful woman who had about her a gracefulness that would stay with her until the end.

"Come along then, my darlings, for our supper guests will arrive very shortly. Your Aunt Matilda will be pleased with both of you, I am sure. And Amabel," she said, turning to the younger, "all I ask is that you enjoy yourself and remember to smile sweetly should some unfortunate gentleman tread on your toes."

Harriet had exaggerated a little when intimating to Mr Chigwell that the party was to be a small one. However, fewer than ten people had been invited to the supper which preceded the main event. All were known to Amabel, the numbers being made up of Sarah and Matthew Carstairs, Elizabeth and Cornelius Ware and their daughter, Lady Sawcroft and finally Mr Gil Carstairs and Major Brew Ware. The Lambert ladies brought the total to eleven. Not the best number, and fewer men were seated around the table than ladies, but with Louisa at the head and Lady Sawcroft at the foot the discrepancy seemed not to be noticed, and certainly it had no detrimental impact on those who attended.

Harriet, whose task it had been to arrange the seating, had been careful to put Cornelius Ware at her mother's right hand while his son, at as great a distance as was possible, was left to entertain Aunt Matilda. While they had maintained a level of civility in the days since their discussion, conversation did not flow easily between the squire and the major, but Harriet had done her best and to good effect.

Since all were well-known to each other, formality was soon abandoned, initially provoking a raised eyebrow from Lady Sawcroft. Brew soon charmed her and when he addressed Gil Carstairs, on the other side of the table and two chairs along, she condescended enough to add her own comments. Very soon any vestige of loftiness was discarded and she was thoroughly entertained. Harriet had kindly placed her sister next to Gil Carstairs, thus ensuring that when it was time to welcome those visitors who were to attend the ball itself, Amabel would be as relaxed as possible.

Though not on a grand scale, there were people in sufficient numbers to justify the term 'squeeze', as Louisa had hoped. When all had been greeted and had adjourned to the ballroom, the tone was set for the evening. As the most senior invited male guest, it was Matthew Carstairs who claimed Amabel for the first dance, but his son was next to solicit her hand. By the time the musicians struck up their instruments for the waltz it was evident that this party, early in the season though it was, would stand as an example for those to follow.

It was well into the evening, and Brew had plucked some lemonade from a tray held by a passing waiter and handed it to Harriet. She accepted it gratefully.

"It isn't often that I curse my legacy from the war, Miss Lambert, but I would dearly love to be able to invite you to stand up with me," he said.

"I would far rather you sat beside me and that we had an opportunity to talk. I would be telling less than the truth if I said I didn't like to whirl around the floor as much as the next person, but every now and then one requires a little respite, don't you think? In fact, it is so hot in here I would deem it a favour if you would escort me into the garden. You must tell me what you think of the decorations, for they were my particular task."

As they stepped out, Brew marvelled at this woman who had never drawn embarrassed attention to his disability. They settled down on a bench situated next to a small water feature with a statue of a nymph beside it.

"My mother, I know, is grateful to yours for inviting Rebecca to your sister's ball. Everyone has been exceedingly kind. Had I returned to England earlier and been reunited with my family sooner, I might have been able to give a ball in her honour. But to tell you the truth, I think she prefers this gentler way of being introduced into society. For all her spirit when in the company of those with whom she's acquainted, she is a modest girl and doesn't, I believe, like to put herself forward."

"Amabel is the same. She was at sixes and sevens this morning, and all in anticipation of being the centre of attention."

"And yet she is the picture of calm self-assurance."

Harriet laughed. "On the outside, perhaps. Inside I make no doubt she is trembling like a leaf. We must be grateful your friend stays so close to her side. When she is with him, she assumes a confidence not habitual to her."

"They are alike then in that respect, our sisters. No doubt tomorrow each will be pouring their thoughts and emotions into their mothers' ears. I almost wish I could be there to hear what Becca has to say," Brew said with a slightly twisted smile.

"Since thus far neither has been without a dance partner, I expect they will have much to say."

"Will you be involved in the aftermath of the party, Miss Lambert, or can I persuade you to take a drive with me in the park tomorrow?"

"I expect my mother would like me to remain here," Harriet said, her tone briefly reflecting Brew's own disappointment, before she went on, "but if you should be free the following day I would be delighted."

His smile returned once more.

CHAPTER THIRTEEN

Their guests all having departed, the three Lambert ladies surveyed the now less than perfectly presented ballroom, chairs having been moved, glasses having been placed on pieces of occasional furniture, and one or two of the multitude of candles beginning to splutter in their sockets. They adjourned to the withdrawing room, each sinking gratefully into a comfortable chair. Louisa kicked off her slippers and rested her feet on a stool.

"Well, I really don't know if I'm glad that's over or not. It all went rather well, didn't it, my dears?"

"Yes, Mama, and no small thanks to you and Harry for making it so. I swear there wasn't a single thing I would have changed. From the moment Mr Carstairs led me onto the floor I was as relaxed as could be, something I hadn't anticipated at all."

"And to which Mr Carstairs might you be referring, dearest?" Harriet teased.

"Don't laugh at me, Harry. I was talking about Mr Matthew Carstairs, obviously, though naturally I was excessively happy in his son's company. You can neither of you have any doubt how much I admire him."

"Well, there's no need for you to cry," her mother said as she saw the ready tears in her daughter's eyes. "It must be evident to the world that he feels the same about you, though he makes a valiant effort to hide it, and I honour him for that. I am strongly of the opinion that you will soon be receiving an offer from him, and that he has only held back thus far while you have been making your way into society."

"And," Harriet added, "I must compliment you on not allowing your gaze to follow him about the room. Your behaviour tonight was impeccable; you gave your complete attention to each of the guests with whom you were engaged. I couldn't be more proud."

This last was too much for young Amabel and the tears she'd been holding back overflowed, but her sparkling blue eyes were shining with happiness. "I hope you are right, both of you. This has been the best evening of my life but, you know, I suddenly find myself overwhelmingly tired. Would you mind very much if I retired now?"

Her mother smiled sympathetically. "I think we should all do the same."

In spite of her tiredness, Harriet lay awake until the early hours trying to analyse her feelings for Brew Ware. She was no fool. She acknowledged that she was strongly drawn to him and that the emotions she was experiencing were quite different from those she had felt for John Downing. These were much gentler and less passionate, but she had to admit that he was fast becoming the first person she thought of upon waking.

In Duke Street, Elizabeth Ware listened to her daughter expressing her own thoughts about the evening. They were in Becca's bedchamber, Cornelius having bid them goodnight earlier and retired. Rebecca was sitting in bed with her knees drawn up and the covers pulled under her chin. Her mother surveyed her from the comfort of a bergère armchair with back and armrests upholstered in gold.

"We are indebted to Louisa Lambert, are we not, my child? And to Sarah and Matthew. They have introduced you to the ton, and after tonight I believe we can expect even more morning callers than before. You are indeed a fortunate young woman."

"Yes, Mama, and had it not been for the legacy left to me for that very reason, we would still be at Austerly and I would yet be dreaming."

"Of your prince?" her mother asked with an understanding smile.

"No, that dream is long gone, but I never thought to be able to come to London, to meet so many kind people, to see my brother again and for him to take me to the theatre. All these things seemed until recently to be impossible. And, not knowing of my godmother's legacy until a few short months ago, how could I ever have believed it might one day happen? Why did you not tell me when she passed away?"

Elizabeth folded her hands in her lap and looked down at her intertwined fingers. It was a fair enough question, for Becca had certainly been of an age to understand. She raised her eyes to look directly at her daughter. "I had my reasons."

"Papa!"

"As you say, Papa."

"But the choice was not his, surely."

"Imagine if you will, Rebecca. Your father was unable to fund this trip. How much more of a blow to him was it that your godmother could and would do so? I should not say it, but Papa has many … eccentricities. But one thing he has in abundance — too much, if you ask me — is his pride. It took me many months, firstly to summon up the courage to broach the subject and then, little by little, to wear down his resistance. Don't misunderstand me. He was as keen as I that you should have your opportunity. It was reconciling himself to the fact that he was not the one to provide that chance that rankled him."

"Was he then so hard to persuade?"

"Let me just say that I took my time. Eventually, of course, he saw that it was inevitable. For one, it would go against the terms of your godmother's will if he did not comply and for another, well, I doubt you can remember the man he was before Nancy's dreadful accident. You were the light of his life, all of you. There was never a father more proud of his children than Cornelius. Of course he wants you to have your moment. But it took time. That is why it is happening only now and not when you reached the age of eighteen shortly after your godmother's death."

"To tell you the truth, Mama, I am more than happy it is now. Having led so sheltered a life, I am unsure as to how I might have coped at so tender an age. But, and this is far more to the point, Brew was not then back from France. His being here now plays such a huge part in the whole. You don't think he will go away again, do you?"

Elizabeth didn't and said so. "While he is not on the best of terms with your father, you may observe from this evening that they are able to meet in company and be civil to each other. There is a long way to go, but I see no reason why Brew should leave. Has he not told us of his hope to restore Austerly to its former glory? I feel sure he is focused on this above all else. No, he will not go away again."

"But tonight they spoke only for a moment, for the sake of appearance. Papa went as soon as he could to the card room and was not seen again for the rest of the evening."

Elizabeth laughed and the tension in Becca's shoulders relaxed in response. Mama could not be thus if things were bad. "You must know your father well enough to realise he would have sought refuge in the card room whether Brew had been there or not." Elizabeth then changed the subject. "There were several young men who were seeking you out this evening. Is there one for whom you might have a preference?"

Rebecca replied that all had been charming, but there were none for whom she felt she might form an attachment. What she did not confide was that there was such a man elsewhere — but Dorian Fletcher had not been invited to Amabel Lambert's ball.

There was no feeling of anti-climax in Hay Hill following the ball. If anything, the frisson of excitement that had preceded it was further magnified when on the following day Mr Gil Carstairs offered Miss Amabel Lambert his hand and his heart. Paying an early visit, he was fortunate to find Mrs Lambert alone, her daughters being occupied elsewhere. With old-fashioned courtesy, he asked to be allowed to pay his addresses to Amabel.

"I am aware we have been acquainted only a few short weeks, but I knew immediately. I would beg you..." He stopped mid-sentence when Louisa raised her hand.

"You need not go on. I ask only that my daughter be happy with her chosen partner, and I do not hesitate to say that it is evident to me that she is most happy in your company. She will be here shortly, and I shall contrive to leave you alone together so you may have your say."

Gil would have said more but it was at that point that Harriet and Amabel came into the morning room, the younger pulling up short when she saw who was there.

"Come in, girls. Mr Carstairs is anxious to speak with Amabel. I suggest, sir, that you escort her to the garden, where you will be undisturbed," she said, smiling inwardly as the colour fled from Amabel's face to be replaced almost immediately with a warm flush which did nothing to detract from her appearance.

Harriet, who had followed her sister into the room, stood aside to let the couple pass before closing the door behind them. She moved straight away to grasp her mother's hands. "They will be so happy, don't you think, Mama? Poor Gil, I watched him yesterday evening, almost in agony as one young man after another led my sister onto the floor."

"Indeed they will. I am fairly certain he had no intention of declaring himself for a while yet. Perhaps, as you say, the sight of other men paying court to her was all that was needed to prompt him to take action."

Gil was at that moment saying as much to Amabel. He had led her to the same spot where Harriet and Brew had retired the previous evening during the ball. He settled her onto the bench and sat beside her before causing her alarm by leaping almost immediately to his feet. Then he dropped to one knee and she felt only breathless anticipation.

"Miss Lambert. Amabel. You must know how I feel about you. Such anguish it was yesterday to watch one after another dancing with you and, seeing you in the arms of another as you twirled around the room in the waltz, well, I can stand it no longer. Put me out of my torment and say you'll be mine."

She laid trembling fingers on his shoulder, her eyes sparkling as her greatest wish had come true. "Gil, nothing would give me greater honour than to be your wife. Of course I will marry you. I only pray I can make you as happy as you have made me."

He rose and pulled Amabel to her feet, folding her into his arms before kissing her gently. He felt her lips quiver beneath his and with a supreme effort drew back, not wanting to frighten her. "We must be married immediately," he said.

She giggled. "I think perhaps we might wait a day or two, do you not?" she asked. "There are, after all, one or two arrangements to be made."

"No, but, well, you know what I mean, my darling," he said, distractedly raking his hand through his hair. "May we go now and break the news to your mother and sister? Not that I think they will be surprised. And then I must leave you to go and inform my parents. Send a notice to the *Morning Post*. Have the banns proclaimed. Shall we be married at St George's in Hanover Square? Where would you like to go on your honeymoon? So many things to think about and to do."

Gil's excitement was infectious, but she merely said, "Let us first go to my mother. Then you to Mr and Mrs Carstairs. Then," she added shyly, "come back to me and we shall discuss how to proceed."

He tucked her hand in his arm and they returned to the morning room.

Sarah and Matthew Carstairs were no more surprised at the betrothal than Louisa Lambert had been, nor indeed was Brew Ware when Gil returned to Grosvenor Square just as the major was about to dine. Gil burst into the room quite evidently so big with news that Brew asked, "Don't tell me, man, your horse has come home first and you have won a fortune."

"I have won something far better than a fortune, let me tell you. This morning I returned to Hay Hill and I am happy to tell you that Amabel has consented to become my wife. What a day this has been," Gil said, throwing himself enthusiastically into a chair. "I must say, that looks good," he added, eyeing his host's plate and looking at the variety of dishes that had been placed on the table.

"Then I suggest you take a plate from the dresser over there and join me. There is more than enough for two. And while we are eating, you can tell me all about it. I couldn't be happier for you. I have no doubt you and Miss Lambert will deal delightfully. When is the wedding to take place?"

"Not soon enough for me. You wouldn't believe how many details there are to take care of. My parents have been informed. I have today been to St George's so that the banns may be read. We must wait three weeks!" he groaned, as though the prospect of such a time was agonising. "An announcement has been placed in the press, and I'm afraid I will be leaving Grosvenor Square. I must hire a house for my wife, for there is no knowing when my mother will take it upon herself to spend more time in London, and I think it grossly unfair to expect the ladies to reside under the same roof."

"Very wise. Do you mean to make the capital your permanent home?"

"Not at all, but it is best to have something in place. Amabel and I will return to Langborne — we discussed it this afternoon. There are two or three properties on the estate which would be suitable for us, and I plan to take her there as soon as we are returned from our honeymoon. And that's another thing. She has a hankering to visit Paris. Thanks to you I'm pretty familiar with the place, so we're to go there after the wedding. I must say, I like the way your chef has of preparing this joint," he added, carving some more beef and placing it on his plate.

Brew leaned back in his chair and watched as his childhood friend outlined plans for the future. They had shared much in the past, and he found himself wishing for his own happy ending. The prospect seemed unlikely, given that the only woman for whom he had ever felt such sentiments seemed still to be mourning her lost love. He had admitted to himself that his feelings for Harriet were far stronger than those of friendship.

With his ebullient friend silenced for a moment by his appreciation of the fine food of which he was partaking enthusiastically, Brew raised the subject of his proposed drive the next day with Amabel's sister. "Perhaps you and she would care to join us again, though we go no further than the park this time."

"An excellent plan. I shall send a note to Hay Hill immediately." All at once Gil became serious. "We've had little opportunity to talk about the ball, you and I. Did things go well with your father?"

Brew contemplated the glass of wine he had been about to raise to his lips. "Well? I think we are a long way from well, but at least he did not embarrass my family or our hostess. I am firmly of the opinion that we can do no better than leave him to the direction of your own father. Matthew has been a good friend and has shown an understanding towards my sire that I would not have believed possible. If anyone can lead him, for he will most certainly not be driven, it will be he. In the meantime, the ice has been broken. I can only hope it will soon begin to melt."

CHAPTER FOURTEEN

Seeing his mother walking with his sister in the park, Brew pulled up his carriage the next day to greet them. With Walter standing at the horses' heads, all four occupants descended to the drive and Elizabeth and Rebecca had an opportunity to convey their good wishes to the newly betrothed couple. The major managed a quiet word with his mother, telling her of his intention to visit later in the day if she was to be at home.

"Yes, we are to attend a soirée this evening at the kind invitation of yet another of Sarah's friends, but we have no particular plans until then, once we have returned from our walk."

"Does my father go too?"

"Yes, Matthew has insisted. He told Cornelius he had no intention of escorting three women on his own, for we are to go with him and Sarah, and it seems your father recognised the age old appeal of one man to another."

Brew laughed and said he knew exactly what she meant, but a slight crease furrowed his brow. "I hope we may exchange more than two words when I come to Duke Street later on. Does he mention me at all, Mama?"

The dropping of her eyes told him all he needed to know.

"Ah well, perhaps it was too much to hope for so soon. I see that fellow Fletcher is dancing attendance on my sister," he added, looking speculative as the man approached with the obvious intention of once more making Rebecca the object of his gallantry. "Does he make a nuisance of himself?"

"Not at all. He is absolutely charming. I hear a slight edge in your voice, Brew. Do you not like him?"

"I hardly know him, but I do know something of his circumstances and I don't like to see him dangling after Becca. The word is that he finds himself on the rocks and is hanging out for a rich wife, so why he's paying court to her I do not know."

Elizabeth thought he was being overly cynical and said so.

"Believe me, Mama, I would that I was wrong. There can be no doubt my sister is developing a tendre for him, though she hides it well. I mention it only so that you should be forewarned. She may be reading more into what might after all be no more than a mild flirtation on his part, but I would ask that you inform me if you have any qualms. I make no doubt I could, if necessary, nip things in the bud."

His mother laughed, but it was not happy laughter. "I can see now why you were so successful in your occupation. You have the habit of mustering your troops to your will."

The group dispersed soon after, but not before Brew had had an opportunity to study his sister. There could be no doubt. Rebecca was smitten, and either he was a very good actor or the same could be said for Dorian Fletcher. Such was the major's distraction that, once more taking up the reins, his attention was called upon by Harriet, who was moved to ask if anything was disturbing him.

"Not at all," he said, pulling himself together. "Those two are *aux anges*, are they not?" he continued, gesturing over his shoulder to Amabel and Gil seated behind them. "I can only pray that one day you will be able to set aside your own loss and be similarly circumstanced."

Harriet's eyes flew to his face, shock transforming her own features. "What?"

"I beg your pardon. I shouldn't have spoken so. You have confided in me about Downing, and I believe he is still often in your thoughts. Forgive me. Is it not so?"

She hardly knew how to respond. It was true she thought of John, but always in her past, not her present. She did not want to appear callous in the major's eyes, but she had moved on and told him so. "I will always remember him with great affection but it has, after all, been three years. You must not think I am still in mourning." Harriet stopped, uncertain as to how to continue, but she could not know how much hope her words had given her companion.

"I am glad it is so." Brew changed the subject. "I hope you don't think I have overstepped the mark, but I haven't forgotten our conversation in Richmond Park. It has been brought to my notice that there is a fine mare for sale that might suit you while you are in London. I remember you saying how occupied you were with your sister's ball, but that is gone by and perhaps you might now have the opportunity to indulge yourself. Would you like me to arrange for you to see her? She is currently the mount of the wife of a friend. They are moving abroad and wishful of selling their stable."

Harriet's anxiety disappeared in her excitement and they were comfortable once more. She begged that he should do so and promised to hold herself ready, whatever day or time should be convenient.

"Then I shall see what I can do, Miss Lambert. And here we are, back in Hay Hill. I hope to have the pleasure of seeing you again soon."

Two hours later, Major Ware presented himself at the house in Duke Street to find all three members of his family at home and seated in the drawing room. He was surprised to see on his father's face a look not of anger or dismissal but more a quizzical expression that he could not for the moment decipher. However, after Brew had greeted his mother and sister, his father stood up and said, "A word with you, boy." He then walked abruptly from the room.

Feeling like a child caught in a misdemeanour, Brew trailed after the squire, his limp a little more pronounced as it always was when he became agitated. Cornelius Ware stood by the hearth in the library, a tall man with an imposing figure which not even the ravages of time and circumstance had contrived to disguise. The haggard look his son had noted outside White's had to some extent dissipated. There was something more about him of the man Brew remembered from his childhood.

"Sit down, if you wish," he was invited, but the major, familiar with tactical manoeuvres, knew at once this would cause him to feel at a disadvantage and went instead to stand by the window. There was silence for a few moments as each sized the other up, the younger waiting patiently for his parent to speak.

"I have come by some surprising information," Cornelius began. "It would seem that not only did you have a successful career in the army but that you have been busy since the end of the war acquiring for yourself no small fortune. Is that correct?"

"It is, sir."

"And you didn't think to mention it to me?"

Brew's sense of humour asserted itself and he smiled, to the evident surprise of his father. "I have been hard put to say anything to you for fear you would thrust my words down my throat. It is no secret, nor have I tried to make it so. That you were unaware of my circumstances stems only from the fact that I have had no opportunity to discuss them with you. May I say I am glad of the chance to do so now."

"Impudent cub! To whom do you think you are talking?"

"Why, to you, sir. You must admit you haven't made it easy." His words hung in the air for a moment, but the grin which he could not keep from his face took the sting out of them.

There was the glimmer of a response from Cornelius. His features softened, almost imperceptibly but enough for Brew to relax. He believed there was a chance at last that they might reach an understanding.

"Why don't I fetch a bottle of burgundy and we can sit down and discuss it now?" suggested Brew. He didn't wait for an answer but followed the question with the deed. As he came back into the room, he saw that his father had sat at the table and was waiting expectantly. Brew sat opposite and poured each of them a glass. Holding his own up to the light, he contemplated that the coming few minutes might determine the whole of his future relationship with the squire.

"I will begin, if you like, by relating all that has happened since I left Austerly."

Cornelius said nothing but leaned back in his chair, his fingers nursing the stem of his glass. Crossing one leg over the other, he prepared himself to listen.

"I was wrong to run away the way I did," Brew began. "I said as much in my letter to you. The only excuse I can make is that of immaturity. I was mad for the army. That you already know, and I am happy to say that my time in the service of my country fulfilled all my boyhood dreams." He paused, knowing what he had to say next would not be what his parent wished to hear. "I was aware that you were in no position to purchase a commission for me. I believe you thought I resented the fact. It wasn't the case. What I bore a grudge about for so many years was that you wouldn't discuss the matter with me. But then, we didn't discuss anything, did we?"

Cornelius's face had paled but still he didn't speak.

"Allow me to go back even further, if you will. In hindsight I can see that when I told you of my fears about the well, you had little or no opportunity to act upon them before Nancy returned there. I know that now. I didn't then. And my own guilt — yes, I too blamed myself — was turned upon you. It is only with the passage of time that I can see that neither of us was at fault. Nancy's death was no more or less than a tragic accident, and for us to have carried such bitterness all these years only makes it more so."

Cornelius raised his glass to bloodless lips.

"Let me then move on. You are aware, for I have told you, that I attained my majority, but when the war was over I had no desire to serve in a peacetime army. With no home to return to, I remained in France. Lady Luck smiled upon me. I had some skill with the cards and before long, my fortunes had changed."

At last his father spoke. "It isn't what I would have chosen for you."

Brew grinned. "Perhaps not, but you must confess it's damned convenient, sir. It was during this time that I began to think more of home. I realised the loss of my sister had changed all our lives, but I thought that maybe our fractured family might once again come together. Eventually, and by now a very wealthy man, I returned to England, but I had no idea of what my reception might be if I came back into Lincolnshire. So I wrote to you instead, and when you did not reply I was at a loss as to know what to do next. And then there was that awful meeting outside White's. Well, to tell you the truth I was prepared to chuck the whole thing in.

Fortunately Gil Carstairs has been at my right hand this whole time, as I believe Matthew has been at yours."

"No man ever had a truer friend. So, what are your plans now, if I may ask?"

Brew tossed back the rest of his drink and refilled both their glasses. He knew he was on shaky ground. "That very much depends on you, sir. If you would permit, I should like to return to Austerly and see if I cannot help with its restoration. It is at present in a sad state of repair."

"You have been there?"

"It was my right as your heir."

All at once the older man's shoulders slumped. It was a sad sight for his son. "It is not from choice that your inheritance is in its current state," said Cornelius. "I had, have always had, the desire but not the means to make reparation."

"I am fully conscious of the fact. But I do have the means and, if you would allow me, it is a task we could embark upon together."

"I imagine I have little choice in the matter. Do what you will, then. I would wish it for your mother if not for myself."

Brew had only one stipulation and now was not the time to voice it. He was determined that all signs of the well should be removed and it was something he would insist upon, but not today. They had covered a lot of ground, and the result had been far in excess of anything he could have hoped for. For the moment it was more than enough.

Amabel was not the only Lambert lady to receive an offer. At the very moment Brew was engaging with his father, Harriet was receiving a proposal from Mr Chigwell, he of the striped waistcoats. She was rather touched by it and had no desire afterwards to scoff at him or to share the details with her family — and certainly not with Major Ware, to whom she had previously derided him. A new side was seen of this man whom she all at once perceived used his wardrobe to cover his feelings of inadequacy.

"I come to congratulate you on the betrothal of your sister, Miss Lambert. I am certain you are all delighted that she is to enter into the happy state of matrimony." Mr Chigwell paused and took a deep breath before continuing, almost doggedly, Harriet thought. "You must know by now that I am not indifferent to you. It has for some time been my wish that you and I might form an alliance. In short, I would beg you to do me the honour of becoming my wife."

There was no pomposity in his declaration. It was placed before her with a simplicity which only served to accentuate his sincerity. Thus it was with a pang that she had to refuse him, though she did so as gently as she could.

"You honour me more than I can say, sir. Believe me when I tell you that I truly value your friendship, but I do not have those deeper feelings to which you allude. I would not dishonour you, nor indeed any man, by pretending to be affected by sentiments which I do not hold. Forgive me, but I must decline your very kind offer."

"I feared as much. I had allowed myself to hope but, well, you will I pray allow me to continue nonetheless to engage with you when we meet. I must tell you that for me you light up any room you enter, and if I cannot be your husband I would desire at least to remain your friend. I wish you only well. Please convey my best wishes to your family."

He stayed no longer and Harriet sat alone for a while after he had gone, reflecting upon how wrong she had been in her judgement and what a nice man he was. She hoped that in time he would find another woman to whom he could give his love.

She resolved not in future to judge a person by his or her appearance. When she joined her mother, Amabel having gone for a walk with Gil, Louisa asked immediately if the anticipated offer had been made.

"It has, Mama, and with great dignity. I find I have been mistaken in his character and will strive to be more perceptive in the future. I was too quick to pass judgement. Beneath all his bravado, Mr Chigwell is a gentle man. I wish him well, though I cannot marry him."

Her mother looked at her thoughtfully. She was aware that there was much Harriet kept to herself. She judged it was time to ask her a question. "Do you carry a flame still for John Downing, dearest?"

"No, Mama, merely the memory of what might have been. And to answer the next question, yes, I would like to be married someday. I hope to be as lucky as my sister and to meet a man who will fulfil that dream. In the meantime, I am quite content."

"Then I am satisfied."

Louisa let it rest there. Harriet's company was as much sought as a mother could wish. There was rarely a time at any function when there was not someone paying court to her, and if she did sit out a dance it was usually because she was deep in conversation, often with Major Ware, whom Mrs Lambert knew could not participate in that activity. Far more private than her younger sister, Louisa knew that to question Harriet further would be a fruitless exercise. But she did wonder, and most certainly she did not despair.

CHAPTER FIFTEEN

Harriet could scarcely contain her excitement when, the very next day, Major Ware called and asked if she might be free to inspect the horse he had mentioned to her.

"Mrs Somerfield has informed me that she is to ride in the park this morning, and you might like to see Brandy being put through his paces."

"I should like that above all things. Will you just give me time to fetch my pelisse, if you please? Do we walk to the park?"

"No, my carriage is waiting outside. My team will be fine for a while. Walter will walk them if need be. Do not rush yourself, Miss Lambert."

But rush she did. She was a keen rider and had missed the sport more than she cared to admit but with Amabel's ball having taken place, followed so speedily by her betrothal to Mr Carstairs, the call upon Harriet's time at home was no longer so pressing. She could indulge herself in a way she had thus far been unable to.

"Do you go to the Fieldstones' soirée tomorrow, Major?" Louisa was asking Brew as Harriet re-entered the drawing room.

"I do and am looking forward to it immensely. It will be my last social occasion in town for a while, Mrs Lambert, as I am off the following day to my family home in Lincolnshire."

An unbidden sense of dismay settled upon Harriet as she admitted to herself how much she would miss his company. Also, should Brandy prove to be suitable, she had anticipated that on occasion the major would be her riding companion.

These thoughts were immediately superseded by a desire to know what had suddenly called him back to Austerly. All this went through her mind while he stood aside to hold the door open for her, and then her heart went head about heels as he glanced down at her with such a smile as to set her pulses racing.

Harriet had regained her composure by the time she was seated next to Brew in the carriage. As he took up the reins, she asked whether he proposed to make a long stay in the country.

"Not above a week, I believe. But I must tell you, for you are aware of our estrangement, that I have spoken to my father since last we met, and we have to some degree reached a new understanding. He is to travel with me to Austerly, where we are to meet with his steward. It is my fervent wish that we can come to some agreement regarding the state of the place, for it has been sadly neglected through no fault of the squire's. I hope very much that the work may be undertaken speedily, for it will make my mother so much more comfortable."

"And Mrs Ware and Rebecca, do they remain in London in the meantime?"

Brew laughed. "Indeed, it would be cruel of me to drag my mother, and therefore my sister, away at this time. Becca is enjoying her first season here and would, I believe, protest strongly were she to be removed."

"Then I shall look forward to your return and, if Brandy proves to be a suitable mount for me, I rely on your companionship when out riding. When in Kent I have no compunction in tearing around the countryside unaccompanied, but it would not do in London, although I will of course hire a groom. But one cannot derive the same enjoyment as when in the company of a friend, don't you think?"

It was perhaps a little forward for her to voice her sentiments so plainly, but Harriet felt their friendship to be sufficiently established for her not to appear to be a pushing sort of woman. Brew appeared delighted that she wished to spend time with him in such a way and professed the hope that she and the gelding would prove to be compatible. He took his eyes off the road ahead to smile at her again, which once more caused her insides to flutter in a rather pleasant and exciting manner.

With an ease which masked the skill required, the major swung his carriage into the park and it wasn't long before he brought it to a halt at the sight of a couple approaching from the other direction. Mr and Mrs Somerfield reined in beside them and introductions were made as Harriet and Brew descended to the drive and the two riders dismounted. Harriet liked Diana Somerfield on sight, a woman of perhaps five and thirty, slight of build and in complete contrast to her giant of a husband.

"You must see how unsuited we are, Miss Lambert, for I must be forever raising my head if I wish to speak to Eustace when we ride, or indeed at any time," she said with a warm smile that showed immediately how great was her regard for him. "With his mount standing a whole hand higher than mine, we cut a curious picture when out together, but both horses are so well-mannered as to put up with us and each other. We shall be sorry to part with them, and would not do so if not out of necessity."

"I understand entirely, Mrs Somerfield. One forms a bond, does one not? My own favourite remains in Kent but I must assure you that, should Brandy and I suit, there is room in my heart for both and I will take him with me when I return. Yes, sir, I mean you," she laughed as the horse, whose neck she had been stroking, turned his head to nuzzle her hand. He was a neat bay, but what attracted her most was his evident good temperament.

"A pity you are not dressed for riding, Miss Lambert, but if you would care to return tomorrow suitably attired, you might perhaps like to take a turn about the park before deciding whether or not you think Brandy is for you. Perhaps the major can once more escort you."

"That is kind of you indeed. I have not brought my habit with me to London, but I'm certain I can find something more suitable to wear."

Both women looked enquiringly at Brew, who had been standing to one side talking to Eustace Somerfield while at the same time following their conversation.

"I should be delighted. Shall we say twelve o'clock?"

It was agreed and they parted company, Harriet happy in the knowledge that she would soon have her own mount, sure as she was that she and Brandy would deal well together. She was also delighted that she would at least have the opportunity to spend some more time in the major's company, both in the morning and at the Fieldstones' soirée. She no longer questioned her feelings. Slowly but surely, the major had won her heart. She knew he was fond of her but had no notion as to whether or not he nurtured those more tender feelings for her. She knew only that she would miss him dreadfully while he was away.

Brew had been surprised when his father had elected to go with him to Austerly. The prospect of travelling together in a closed carriage for hours on end filled him with apprehension, but he was of the opinion it was the only option to ensure his parent's comfort in so far as he was able. They set out early on the designated day, taking leave of his mother and sister and bidding them enjoy themselves while their menfolk were away.

Cornelius settled back against the squabs and regarded his son with an unreadable expression before remarking, "You may have wondered why I wished to come with you. It is not, as you might suppose, that I don't trust you, but more that I am naturally curious to hear what you and Pullman might come up with. You will forgive me, and do not take it personally, if I don't indulge in conversation with you. I do not travel well and prefer to close my eyes against the swaying of the carriage."

"Certainly, sir. You must do whatever suits you best. I am of much the same opinion myself and prefer not to partake of idle chatter."

He then sat back in his own corner and smiled to himself at the prospect of idle chatter with his father. In his mind the two definitely did not go together. He turned his thoughts instead to the previous day. To no-one's surprise, Harriet and Brandy had suited each other well, and he admitted to himself that watching her and the pleasure that riding gave her filled him with a sense of well-being. A deal had been struck and arrangements had been made for the gelding to be transferred without delay, Diana Somerfield having asserted that if she had to part with him, it had to be quick. Later that evening at the Fieldstones' soirée, his heartstrings had been pulled when Harriet had looked wistfully at him and voiced her disappointment that he would not be able to ride out with her for a while. "But I hope that by the time you return to London, he and I shall have become better acquainted and you will not be sorry to have recommended me to Mrs Somerfield," she'd added.

"You forget, Miss Lambert, that I watched you ride this morning. I can have no regrets." He had been on the point of declaring himself when he'd realised that this was not the time, not when he was leaving the next morning.

And so it was that he was now whiling away the hours, not in anticipation of the week ahead but beyond, to when he would return to London. He decided it was time to chance his luck. Would she have him? He could not know, but neither could he wait any longer to find out.

By the time he and his father reached the appointed stop for the night, the squire was alarmingly pale and Brew realised that such a journey had been quite an ordeal for him. He was not a young man and sitting hour upon hour and, on occasion, being jolted about had pulled him. He chose to dine quietly in his room and Brew took no offence, realising that his father needed time to himself to recover.

"I wish you goodnight, sir. If you are not feeling up to snuff tomorrow, we can delay our departure and take an extra day."

He spoke with all the compassion Cornelius could have wished for, but the older man said he preferred to cover the ground as quickly as possible and get it over and done with.

"Then I shall see you at breakfast in the morning, Father. I trust you will sleep well."

"Thank you. Goodnight, son."

Brew watched his parent's retreating figure with what felt like a large constriction in his throat. He could not remember when last he had been called son.

To his relief, Cornelius was looking much brighter the next morning and they set off in good time, both much relieved when Austerly came into view and their journey was over.

They had sent word ahead, so all was in readiness for them and the staff showed no surprise at seeing the two of them together. Mrs Gardner had prepared a meal and the two men sat, one at the head and the other at the foot of the table. It was later, when they were drinking their port, that Cornelius looked directly at his son.

"I never thought I would live to see this day." He raised his glass. "We shall do, boy. We shall do. Welcome home."

An unaccustomed prickling caused Brew to run the back of his hand across his eyes.

"I am happier than I can say to be here, Papa." The word felt strange on his lips, but also good. Yes, it definitely felt good.

Harriet, who had sent to Kent for her riding habit at Brew's first mention of seeking a mount for her, could be seen riding every day, sometimes with only her groom in attendance and occasionally with Gil, who also had a love of the sport. She was very fond of her sister's chosen partner and derived much amusement from their conversations, which invariably centred upon the wedding and his plans for his bride's future. With Amabel and Gil so wrapped up in each other, Harriet found herself spending more and more time with Becca at any event where they were both present. The friendship between them flourished, and so Miss Lambert became the recipient of Miss Ware's confidence.

"Do you not consider Mr Fletcher to be a very personable gentleman, Harriet?"

"Indeed I do. I must say I like his style of dress. Quiet and unassuming, but with a certain something about it, don't you think?"

It was evident from the sparkling look she received that Becca did think so and much more besides.

"Are you developing a tendre for him, my dear? He seems, forgive me, a little old for you."

Her companion blushed but asserted, "Mature, not old. I find his company more to my liking than some of the younger men to whom I have been introduced."

"Well, there's no call for you to look so distressed. From what you have said, I understand he is giving you every regard you might wish for."

Becca looked around nervously. Her gaze fell upon her mother, deep in conversation with Louisa. "Mama does not approve of the connection, I fear. She thinks his attentions too marked, for I must tell you he comes to call nearly every day. But I love him, Harriet, and he loves me. We have contrived once or twice to snatch a few moments alone together, and he assures me his heart is mine. Papa would not hear of it, I know. Dorian has no fortune and my father is anxious to see me established in such a way as I should not have to struggle in the manner he and my mother have done."

"Naturally they only want the best for you, Becca," Harriet remarked, by now deeply concerned. Her friend may have been twenty years of age, but this was her first season and she was unaccustomed to moving in such company. If Dorian Fletcher was indeed the gentleman he professed to be, he ought not, in her opinion, to have spoken in such a way to Rebecca but instead should first have approached her father. "Are you certain you have not magnified the extent of his feelings towards you?"

A determined chin was lifted towards her, a look of defiance in her companion's eyes. "No, for he has told me he wishes to marry me."

Harriet's consternation grew. "Then why, if I may ask, has he not applied to your father?"

The bold front disappeared and the shoulders sagged a little. "He is aware my father will not entertain such a proposal. He says we must find another way."

This was serious indeed. Harriet was at a loss as to what to say or do. If only Brew had been in London she could have taken her fears to him. She did not wish to betray her friend, but it seemed that circumstances had gone beyond such a code of honour. To leave Rebecca prey to such a man would be unforgivable. But her father was in Lincolnshire also, and Harriet was loth to approach Elizabeth on the subject. She decided to sleep on the matter and was hard put when Mr Fletcher presented himself a few minutes later even to be civil towards him. His actions had not been those of the gentleman she had supposed him to be.

Compassionate as she felt towards her friend, Harriet could not find it in herself to promote such a match. She consoled herself with the knowledge that Becca was not without protection and that both her father and brother would return to town in a few days. She spoke not a word of her misgivings to Elizabeth, nor did she confide in her mother or her sister. She was consequently filled with dismay when Mrs Ware called on them in Hay Hill one morning just as she was about to go riding with Gil. The poor woman was beside herself and could barely utter the message she'd come to impart.

"Becca! She's gone! Run away. Here," she said, waving a piece of paper. "She left me this note."

Louisa took the letter from her trembling fingers, but Harriet already knew what it contained. However, when her mother read it aloud for Amabel and Gil to hear, her attention was caught by the wording. It seemed that the errant couple had not eloped to Scotland as she had surmised but were on their way to Dover, with the intention of leaving the country for France.

"The scoundrel!" This from Gil, who tore the letter from Louisa's hand and read it again. "Mrs Ware, do you know what time your daughter left the house?"

"I do not. Only that it must have been in the early hours of the morning, for her bed has not been slept in." With that she sank onto a chair and sobbed uncontrollably.

Gil turned to Harriet. "My dear sister. You will forgive me, but I fear we will have to forego our ride this morning. I must take my leave of you."

She nodded her approval. "You're going after them? I will come with you, if you please."

"What! No, it isn't to be thought of."

"No, Gil, you cannot have considered. They are heading into Kent. My home county. If, no, *when* we overtake them it will be necessary to avoid scandal if at all possible. We can take Rebecca to Merivale and say that I had invited her for a visit, that all had been planned. It is known she and I have become close friends, and no-one will think it strange."

Elizabeth stopped sobbing and looked up with the first glimmer of hope in her eyes. "Is it possible? Do you think you can catch them?"

"We'll have a jolly good try," Gil said, excited at the prospect of some action but keen not to let a worried mother think he was enjoying himself.

Amabel clapped her hands together. "Yes, let us go at once," she said.

Harriet touched her arm. "No, my darling, you cannot come. It is common knowledge that you are preparing for your nuptials, and in any case we cannot both leave Mama. You and she may stay here to present an appearance of normality. If Gil and I are careful, no-one will know we left town together. What do you think, Gil? I will have Brandy returned to the stables and we will go by carriage. Much as I would like to ride, it will not do. Can you arrange transport and be back here in one hour? I shall pack a few things and be ready. Our hope must be that we can overtake them before they reach the coast."

Gil turned to his betrothed. "Your sister is right, my love. Stay here with your mother. Mrs Ware will need your support."

He said no more but kissed her hand and strode out of the room. Harriet went to find her maid and to change into more suitable clothing, and within the hour they were on their way.

CHAPTER SIXTEEN

Four days after arriving at Austerly, and following several meetings with their steward, Brew and Cornelius were gradually reaching an understanding. There were some uncomfortable silences between them and not a few clashes when they didn't agree as to the way forward with the house and the estate, but for the most part each was striving to build on what was after all very shaky ground.

"You are not in the driving seat yet, boy. You will do me the courtesy of making your intentions plain before you give any instructions to Pullman," said Cornelius.

"Naturally," Brew said somewhat drily. "I am well aware that I have very little knowledge about the maintenance of a property and its land. I am more than anxious to learn, both from him and from you, sir."

It wasn't lost on either of them that had their relationship been better during Brew's formative years, the situation might have been entirely different. Nonetheless, the younger man was surprised to discover in himself an enthusiasm far above what he had anticipated. The restoration of his inheritance had in his mind been a matter of responsibility and duty, and a homage to his mother. He hadn't expected to feel a thirst for knowledge, or to find that he possessed an aptitude for management.

He realised that the time he had allotted for the trip fell far short of what was necessary and, though his heart was pulling him back to London and to Harriet, his head told him he needed to remain in Lincolnshire for at least another week. He wrote to his mother and asked that she inform Gil of his intentions, as they had an engagement which regretfully had to be cancelled. His hope was that through his friend the news would reach the Lambert household.

Elizabeth's reply came a few days later.

My darling boy

What I have to tell you will come as a shock, I know. There is no way to soften the blow so, to put it plainly, Rebecca has eloped with Mr Fletcher. They have gone not to Gretna Green but to France. Whether or not it is his intention to marry her I cannot know. Her note to me reveals that this is what she believes, but with a man such as that, who can tell? You were obviously right to warn me about him.

Mr Carstairs and Miss Lambert — Miss Harriet Lambert, that is — have set off in pursuit, she having come up with the idea that, should they overtake them in time, they will carry your sister to her home in Kent. The hope is to avoid a scandal by putting it about that this was an arrangement of some standing, for it is common knowledge that the two have become firm friends. Do not, therefore, come rushing back to London. There is nothing you can do for the time being, and I fear the shock would render your father very ill. You may not be aware, but he is not a well man in spite of his attempts to appear to the contrary. Naturally I will write again when I have news but I say again, do not come and on no account tell Cornelius what has occurred. I know you will wish for action and I understand how this will chafe. But if not for your father or me, think of Becca. Things have been kept quiet for the moment. Your appearance and the manner of it would only cause speculation that we can well do without at this point.

Be reassured about me, if you must. The Lamberts and the Carstairs have folded about me. I am not alone and rely on their support.

Mama

It was fortunate indeed that Elizabeth had been so insistent that he stay away, for Brew's every instinct was to return to London. After due consideration, he could see the strength of his mother's argument. He'd had ample time to observe his father during the past several days. The frailty of his health, something he strove so hard to disguise, had become obvious, even to the extent that, when Brew told his sire of his intention to remain another week, Cornelius remarked, "I had already decided to stay here when you leave. To oversee things, you understand."

Brew understood only too well and was happy for the sake of his father's pride that he had been able to find a legitimate explanation for remaining in Lincolnshire. "Shall I tell my mother, or will you write to her yourself?"

"I shall tell her myself. In the meantime, perhaps you could fetch me a glass of brandy. I have one or two things I wish to attend to in the library."

By the time Brew had fulfilled this request and put his head around the door, his father was already fast asleep at his desk, the quill in his hand but the paper blank in front of him. Brew crept into the room and set down the glass before retiring without disturbing him. The frustration of his enforced inactivity didn't sit well with him, and in an effort to rid himself of the fidgets he called for his horse and spent the next two hours riding about the estate. By the time he returned to Austerly, he was feeling calmer but the sense of doom sat heavily upon his shoulders.

Harriet had, for the sake of discretion, entered the carriage which Gil was driving himself but, once clear of the capital, he halted to take her up beside him. The day was fine, and each was anxious to use what opportunity they had to discuss their plans, though everything depended upon them catching the errant couple before they left Dover.

"Tell me the truth, Gil. What are our chances of overtaking them, do you think?"

"I wouldn't lay two farthings on it," he said grimly. "My hope is that, once they arrive at the port, they will be delayed. From what I know of Fletcher, he does not have the means to hire his own transport and must pay for their passage across the Channel in a sailing boat. My own experience tells me that these conveyances rely entirely upon the tides and the prevailing winds. We must pray that conditions today are not in their favour or, more probably, that it will be too late in the day to embark on such a journey."

"Then we must plan for the best outcome. Will you have any difficulty, do you think, in persuading him to give up his hostage, for that is how I look upon her? She is an innocent young woman, and for a man of his standing to take advantage so is unforgivable."

Gil glanced at her, and from his expression she had no doubt that he would be more than willing to take on his adversary and would succeed. He gave her to understand that she need have no doubts on that score.

"Let us move on then to what might happen next. No doubt Becca will not thank us for interfering in this escapade. To her it must seem beyond romantic. We must do what we can to persuade her to return with us. Once that is done, we will go to Merivale, from where she may write to her mother. If she is still determined to marry this man, if that is indeed his intention, then she must be convinced that her parents would prefer her to do so in a way that does not disgrace them all."

"An excellent plan, Harry. And one upon which I cannot for the moment improve. Do you mind if I call you Harry?"

Harriet laughed. "We are soon to be brother and sister, are we not? Only Amabel calls me Harry. I should be delighted if you do so too."

They proceeded in silence for some time, Gil wondering whether to stop and change his horses or simply break their journey to rest them. The decision was taken out of his hands much sooner than he could have imagined when they came upon a vehicle that had cast a wheel and was resting at a strange angle on the side of the road. Naturally Gil pulled up to see if he could help, but they found no-one present and the horses had been removed from their traces and taken away. He drove on a little further until they reached an inn, where he left Harriet holding the reins while he jumped down to enquire after the travellers.

"It is to be hoped that this is not some other unfortunate traveller and that we have after all overtaken our prey," Gil said. "Sit tight. I shall return as soon as I may to let you know."

Anxious though she was, Harriet smiled at her companion's evident enjoyment of the chase and his anticipation of a happy outcome. She had not long to wait. Gil was back in only a few minutes, pain and glee fighting for dominance on his face. Calling for an ostler to take charge of his team, he beckoned her inside, helping her down from the carriage with his left hand, the other obviously being injured. Nevertheless, he laughed and exclaimed, "Planted him a facer. Think I've broken my hand, but never mind that. Miss Ware is in a very distressed state, so I'll take you to her and leave you alone together. She needs a woman, I think. Meantime I'll deal further with that rogue. No hurry, though — he's out cold at the moment."

At this point, having entered the inn, he showed Harriet to a small private room and backed out again, closing the door behind him. As she was undoing the ribbons of her bonnet, Rebecca threw herself at her, sobbing uncontrollably. Harriet let her hat drop and folded her arms around her friend, waiting patiently until the crying was reduced to hiccoughs and large gulps of air.

"Sit down, my dearest, and tell me all about it, if you are able."

"Oh, Harriet, I have been such a fool. I am so glad the carriage cast a wheel, for it has shown Dorian in his true colours. I am so ashamed. He promised marriage and I believed him. All his amiability disappeared when we were forced to stop here, and he became quite angry when I insisted he hire a private room for me. I could see it in his face, but I gave him no choice. And then, oh, Harriet … then, when we were alone, he, he…"

"He tried to force himself upon you?"

"Yes, and when I resisted he told me to stop being missish. How could I have been so wrong about him?"

Harriet knew very well. There was no doubting Fletcher presented an amiable and attractive figure. To one of Becca's age and inexperience, he must have appeared to be the embodiment of her dreams.

"Well, you are rid of him now, and Mr Carstairs and I will take care of you."

Rebecca giggled and said, "You have no idea how satisfying it was to see Gil lay him out. You must know he and I have been friends since childhood, so I know I am safe with him. And then he and the innkeeper dragged Dorian out of the room, but Gil told me you were coming in. I've never been so pleased to see anyone in my life." She grew serious again and the tears began to flow once more. "How am I ever going to live down this scandal?"

"You won't have to, Becca. There will be no scandal. It has all been decided. We will go not to London but to Merivale, for I believe I have told you my home is in Kent. Your mother and mine will give out that I had reason to return there and that you have accompanied me. Only our families and the Carstairs need ever be aware of what has happened."

"But what of Dorian? He might betray me. Oh, Harriet, what am I to do?"

"Exactly as I have said. That man will not bother you again, and certainly he will not wish his own actions to become public. If I know Gil, he will insist that he continues his journey to the Continent and remain there for the foreseeable future, or it will be his own reputation that is torn to shreds, not yours."

In another side room Gil was enjoying himself immensely, though his adversary would never have been able to tell, so hard was his expression. Fletcher was seated on a chair, having come to his senses, but it was evident he was considerably shaken up and was nursing his face with his hand.

"What kind of a blackguard are you to be taking such advantage of an innocent young woman?" Gil demanded, contempt written clear upon his face even as he lounged comfortably with his shoulder to the wall. "You ought to be horsewhipped. I had not thought you would stoop so low."

It seemed no answer was to be forthcoming and they were, in any case, interrupted by a knock on the door and the entry of the landlord, followed by the doctor. With no knowledge of the circumstances, he knew only that he had two people to examine. He first inspected Fletcher, who seemed to be the more urgent of the two, slumped awkwardly as he was.

"Caught you on the chin, did he? I expect you'll have a sore head for a while, but there's no lasting damage. Now, what's up with you, sir?" he asked, turning to Gil.

A hand was proffered, the discolouration witness to its earlier activity.

"Sit down, man. Over here, by the table. That's right. Now, lay your arm flat so I can have a good look."

He spent a while checking Gil over while his patient winced once or twice.

"Painful, is it? I'm not surprised. It will remain that way for a while, but the good news is that you haven't broken anything. You've got some fine bruising there, though. I would suggest putting your arm in a sling to keep it out of harm's way while it heals. But you'll do. Both of you. I wish you good day."

Gil was more relieved than he liked to show, for he'd had no desire to appear at his own wedding with his hand in plaster. He turned back to his antagonist. "Let me tell you what will happen next. You will have no further contact with Miss Ware. For the sake of her reputation, yours too must unfortunately remain intact. I suggest, though it is more in the way of a command, that after you have sorted out the mess you left on the roadside, you continue on your way to Dover and depart for the Continent with all speed. I would not look to see you back in London for the rest of this season and possibly the next as well. If at any time you reveal anything of what has happened today, I shall drag your name through the mud. Do I make myself clear?"

"Completely."

"And you concur?"

"What choice do I have?"

"I am glad you are able to see reason. You will remain in this room until I and my companions have left the inn. The landlord will inform you when we have gone."

He left the room without another word and went to join the ladies, poking his head around the door before entering. "All right if I come in? I thought you might like to know what has happened."

He then filled them in on the details before a frown marred his features, causing Harriet to ask him what was wrong. He told her that it had been his intention to drive them to Merivale, but by reason of his injury he would not be able to handle the reins.

"Then on no account must you attempt to do so," said Harriet. "I am considered to be no mean whip and will undertake to get you both there safely. Fortunately, it's no great distance from here to Merivale, and we will be there comfortably before it gets dark. Do you feel able to go on, Becca?" she asked, turning to her friend.

"Oh yes, yes please."

In hardly more than an hour they had arrived at Merivale. The housekeeper, Mrs Sweet, accepted without question the explanation that Miss Lambert had need to return home and had brought Miss Ware for company.

"I'm sorry I didn't have time to let you all know, but I'm sure Cook will be able to rustle up something for us to eat, for we are all famished," said Harriet, knowing that Mrs Sweet had never been able to resist her engaging smile.

"I'll go and see her now, Miss Lambert, and then I'll arrange for your rooms to be made ready."

The three of them left alone, they decided the most pressing thing was to write letters to their respective mothers telling them of the happy outcome. It was too late to send them today, but at least reassurance might be had by tomorrow for those awaiting news in London. They then sat in the drawing room in front of a fire which Mrs Sweet had caused to be lit. Nobody spoke of their adventure and after a hearty meal they retired early, each of them grateful that the day had ended so well — even Becca, who had lost all fond feelings for Fletcher after his assault upon her. She may have been wondering what her future held, but she knew full well she had escaped a terrible fate.

CHAPTER SEVENTEEN

Elizabeth's first action when she received her daughter's letter was to write again to her son. Much as she would have liked to have travelled straight into Kent to be reunited with her wayward child, she knew it would negate all the good that had been done. Hers would be the task of informing her friends that Becca was spending a few days in the country with Miss Lambert. More urgent was to set Brew's mind at rest.

My dearest boy

Let me at once relieve your anxiety. Your sister is now safely installed at Merivale, where she will remain with Miss Lambert for a few days. She is unharmed. Gil is to return to town, for he has much to do in preparation for the wedding, but he will go to escort the ladies back in one week unless you are returned by then to fulfil that office and bring Becca home.

I have had ample time since you left to consider what you may or may not be doing at Austerly, and I have something to ask of you in the hope that I am not too late. You know of course that from the vantage point of my withdrawing room I am able to look out upon the well. I have come to the realisation that, while for many years it was a cruel and painful reminder of the past, it has over time become a consolation to me. When I look upon it these days it is not with despair, as it used to be, but with a sense of joy in our young girl. It will always remind me of Nancy, but for a long time now this has been in a good way. Therefore, if you haven't already demolished it, I would beg that you leave it where it is. The choice must be yours, of course, for I understand your feelings on this, but you would make me very happy if you would reconsider your original plan.

Enough said. I hope all is well between you and your father. I am busy enough here, but in truth I am keen to have both you and Becca restored to me. She because I feel she must need me more than ever, and you because, well, now that I have you back it seems I cannot get enough of you. You must forgive a doting mother. I smile as I write this because I know you will take my sentiments in good part. Now I must go because Sarah and Matthew are to collect me shortly. We have arranged to meet Louisa Lambert in the park. You see, we are putting on a united front and gathering our strength from each other.

Please convey my love to your father.

Mama

Brew could not but be relieved to receive his mother's letter, and by the time he did so he had reached the decision not to extend his stay in Lincolnshire. His father, tired though he was, seemed to have taken on a new lease of life, entering enthusiastically into discussions with Pullman. It seemed he had accepted his son as benefactor and appreciated his right to be involved. Much had been put in train and Brew felt sufficiently confident to leave the work to go ahead without him. He could return soon enough to oversee the next stage.

Dearest Mama

My father is busying himself about the place and it is my belief that he is enjoying immensely the opportunity of putting things to rights here. He is a renewed man with a fresh purpose. I have therefore decided to return to London but will do so via Merivale to bring my sister back to you. I have written to Gil to inform him that he may remain in town to finalise the plans for his wedding. If Rebecca needs some time to recover from her ordeal and if I am invited to stay, I may remain in Kent for an extra day or two, so I suggest you do not look for me until at least the middle of next week.

I am delighted (but not at all surprised) that Sarah and Matthew have once again taken you under their wing. I will never forget how they cared for me all those years ago. I owe them a debt I can never repay.

I do not know whether you have thought ahead, about what will happen to my sister. Nor do I know how long you planned originally to remain in town. May I say that I'm happy to provide funds, if these are not available to you, for the two of you to remain in Duke Street until the end of the season. I have observed how she has been received by society, and I believe it will not do for her to return home in her present state of mind. My thoughts are that the attention paid to her if she goes out and about will do much to restore her confidence and self-esteem. I write this now so that you have time to consider your situation before I see you again.

Your loving son
Brew

It was not for him to tell his mother how eager he was to set out again. Time and distance had not erased Miss Lambert from his mind, and he looked forward as much to seeing her again as to reassuring his sister that her future had not been jeopardised.

He drove himself south, deciding it would be useful to have a carriage with him at Merivale to convey his sister and, he hoped, Harriet, back to London. He took his time. The weather was fine and the view from his perch far more expansive than any he might have gained from the interior of any other conveyance. By the time he reached the vicinity of Faversham, he found himself in country he had never before visited and he liked the bleakness of the vista. He had despatched François directly to London, thinking it would do him no harm to look after himself for a few days. He did, however, have Walter with him, his talents as a tiger making the journey far easier than it might otherwise have been.

In the middle of the afternoon on a beautiful spring day, he pulled up in front of Merivale House. It was an imposing building of white stone with wide steps leading up to the entrance, on either side of which stood a marble pillar. The whole effect was one of clean lines and he liked it very much. Leaving Walter at the horses' heads, he mounted the steps and rapped on the door, trying to suppress the feeling of excitement at the thought of seeing Harriet again. He was to be disappointed. The door was drawn back to reveal a woman of uncertain age, who he took to be the housekeeper.

She looked enquiringly at him. "Good afternoon, sir. How may I help you?"

"You must forgive me arriving unannounced. Is Miss Lambert at home? I am Major Ware, Miss Ware's brother, who I believe is staying here at present."

The woman opened the door wide and beckoned him inside before saying, "I'm afraid the mistress is from home at the moment. But do come in. I shall arrange for your carriage to be taken to the stables immediately. I'm Mrs Sweet, the housekeeper."

Disappointment was Brew's overwhelming emotion but he hid it well, expressing his gratitude and accepting the offer of refreshment.

"The ladies have gone out riding and won't be back for a while yet," Mrs Sweet explained. "Miss Lambert was delighted to discover a similar love of the sport in her guest, and they have been out every day since they arrived."

Brew wasn't the least surprised and was grateful that the women had a shared passion which he felt sure would have been instrumental in aiding his sister's recovery from her recent ordeal.

Both women were astonished and thrilled to see Brew, though one hid her feelings far better than the other. Rebecca threw her arms about her brother's neck and burst into tears. He comforted her for some moments before declaring, "Have a care, Becca. My supply of cravats is not endless, and I have come into Kent without my valet."

She laughed, brushing away her tears and exclaiming that had she believed him to be such a coxcomb she would never have incommoded him in such a way. Then she grew serious again and begged his forgiveness for all she had put her family through.

"Yours is not the blame, dearest girl. You are young and innocent, and you have been grossly misused. If anyone should be asking to be forgiven it is I, for I suspected what a man he was and I didn't warn you."

Harriet coughed gently and said, "In my opinion, for what it is worth, neither of you was at fault. The onus rests entirely upon one who professed to be a gentleman and took the worst advantage of a girl when his aim — had he truly felt the way he said he did — should have been to protect her."

Brew turned at last to his hostess. "I owe you a debt I cannot repay, Miss Lambert."

"What humbug you do talk, Major," she said with all the ease she habitually felt when in his company. "Tell me, if you will, do you know if Mrs Sweet has prepared a room for you? You will remain, of course."

"I believe she did mention something about preparing a chamber, yes. And thank you."

"Doubtless she will also have spoken to Cook about supper so, if I may, I would propose you and we go and change. Both Becca and I have been making do, my habit having been sent to London when I acquired Brandy and she not having packed hers when she left home. No, don't distress yourself, Becca. I am merely stating facts. You see us both in what we could scrape together for riding. Our horses did us more honour than we did them, that's for sure, but I know they did not mind. Rhapsody was as delighted to see me as I was her and would care not a jot what I wore. I suggest we meet again in an hour and a half, when we may perhaps enjoy a meal together and discuss how to move forward."

When she got to her bedchamber, the first thing Harriet did was peer into the mirror. She was much dishevelled and her hair was all over the place, but on her face was a serene smile. Brew had come and she must be satisfied.

They spoke only of mundane matters during their meal, the constant interruptions from the staff precluding any serious conversation. For the sake of appearance, Harriet asked Brew, "Do you remain long in Kent, Major Ware? I would enjoy the opportunity of showing you some of its delights."

"Not above two or three days, I fear. My mother, I know, is anticipating my sister's return to London. However, I am entirely unfamiliar with the area, which Becca tells me is in parts quite untamed, and most certainly I would like the chance to see it, if you have a suitable mount for me."

"Indeed we do. My father's horse, Apollo, remains with us, for I could not bear to part with him when he passed away. Naturally he is exercised regularly but you will fit each other well, I think, and it will make a nice change for him."

Brew laughed aloud and she looked at him, startled for the moment and with a question on her face. "You are wondering why I laugh. Your first thought is of course for Apollo. A nice change for him. My own comfort comes a poor second, I fear."

An appreciative gleam lit her eyes. "But of course. Would you expect anything else?"

"No, Miss Lambert, I would not."

All this banter enabled Rebecca to relax, and so by the time they adjourned to the drawing room and were sufficiently private to discuss her own situation, she was less apprehensive than she might otherwise have been.

"I cannot tell you what a debt I owe Gil and Harriet, Brew, but I am so very grateful it is you who have come to escort me back to town. I begin to think I might escape censure after all."

"I think you have little if anything to concern yourself about. While Fletcher evidently cared nothing for your reputation, he will most certainly fear for his own. I have no doubt he will remain as silent about this episode as shall we."

"I worry so much that I have disappointed my father."

"Then worry no longer, for he is in ignorance of all that has occurred and all Mama cares for is that you are safe." Brew turned to Harriet, keen to know what her own plans were. "May I have the pleasure of escorting you as well, Miss Lambert, or are you fixed in Kent for the time being?"

"I would appreciate that very much. I am here only on your sister's behalf and must return to London in time for Amabel and Gil's wedding. My own gown is not yet finished and my poor dressmaker will be hard-pressed, I know. There are other things also which need attending to. Would it suit you if we leave the day after tomorrow?"

"Of course. I am at your disposal."

"Then perhaps we may go riding in the morning. It is as well that you go with someone who knows the ground, for it can be treacherous in places. It is bleak, even at this time of the year, but in my opinion it is very beautiful."

Harriet's pride in this place she called home was evident. Didn't Brew feel the same way about Austerly? Left with no doubts about his own feelings, he planned to ask her to marry him as soon as he could. He had no idea if he would be accepted or if she could be tempted away from Kent. That she valued his friendship he knew. But love? He sighed inwardly, for common sense told him that now was not the time to press his suit. What if she rejected him? How awkward it would be when he had undertaken to accompany her back to town. No, he must spare her any difficulty and hope that he might have an opportunity sooner rather than later, for he wanted nothing more than to call her his own.

Becca did not join them the next morning. She made the excuse that she must write to her father — though not, of course, to tell him of recent circumstances. She had covertly observed both her brother and her friend the previous evening and was surprised when she caught each of them in an unguarded moment. The regard in which they held each other could not have been more obvious. Was it more than mere regard? She did not know but considered it would do no harm to give them the opportunity to be alone together for an hour or two.

An hour or two turned into three or four as Harriet took the major first to inspect the stables, which were set slightly apart from the house. It was an impressive block and reflected in what high regard the Lamberts viewed their animals. He met Ben, the head groom, and Arthur, whose duty it was to exercise Rhapsody each day Harriet was away. He saw how animated she became when in her favourite's company and remarked, once they were mounted and on their way, that she was a true countrywoman. She smiled across at him, conversation being easy now they were proceeding at a walking pace.

"You have the right of it there, Major. Don't misunderstand me. I have enjoyed immensely being in town, but coming back here with your sister has proved to me that this is where my heart lies. I shall return as soon as I may following the wedding."

Brew tried hard not to reveal his disappointment and realised that he must, once they were in London, declare himself with all speed before she made the decision to remove herself. In the meantime, he gave himself up to the enjoyment of this wild landscape that she loved so much.

CHAPTER EIGHTEEN

After an early start the next day, Brew had taken Harriet directly to Hay Hill, following which he had restored his sister to their mother a little before sunset. Staying only for a moment to watch their tearful reunion, he went in search of Gil and was grateful to find him at the house in Grosvenor Square, though evidently on the point of departure.

"Stay a while if you would, old boy. There are one or two matters upon which I would like clarification, if you are able to provide it."

"No hurry. I was off to dine at White's but I'm happy to wait, or even to remain here if you like. Not so keen on my own company, but if you're planning on staying in this evening I'm sure your chef can rustle something up for us both."

"Save for catastrophe, I am not taking another step outside today. Are you happy for me to break open a bottle while we wait for supper?"

Gil laughed. "And when have you ever known me to refuse such an offer? There's a fire roaring in the drawing room. The thought of it is rather appealing at the moment."

"To me too. I just hope I don't fall asleep in the chair. How about the wedding? Are the arrangements going well?"

His friend needed no more encouragement and it wasn't until they were settled, each nursing a glass, that Brew was able to turn him from the subject of his nuptials to the one he had in mind.

"Firstly, allow me to thank for your service on behalf of my sister. No, don't protest," he said as Gil put up his hand. "It is the truth, and Heaven only knows where she would be today if you hadn't been on hand to rescue her."

"It was Harriet's idea to take her to Merivale. I must say, that girl has a fine head on her shoulders. I wasn't thinking straight at all at the time; I was just determined to overtake them and bring Becca home."

"Well, everything has certainly turned out for the best, but something has been puzzling me for some time now. Why would Fletcher drag my sister all the way to France when he could have carried her to Gretna Green and done the deed there?"

Gil's face darkened, and for a moment he contemplated his wine before looking directly at Brew. His voice hardened as he spoke. "It's my belief he never had any intention of marrying her. While it's unlikely your father would have looked kindly upon his suit, the fact remains that he didn't even apply to him. I don't know by what means he persuaded your sister to fly with him. Certainly she was convinced of his intention to marry her. But she's a young girl and she was in love with him. You know what these females are like when romance is in the air."

"In short, you believe it was all a ruse to take advantage of her innocence."

"I do. I stand by what I told you some weeks ago. The man's pockets are to let. There's no way he would marry a near-penniless girl, or one at least with such a small dowry as might be bestowed upon your sister. There's no doubt he wanted her, but only on his terms. Eventually he'd have tired of Becca and presumably left her to her fate. He's young enough still to wait a year or two before tying himself to a rich bride."

Brew noticed that Gil had set down his glass and was rubbing one hand with the other. There was, too, a look of grim satisfaction on his face.

"You have an injury, Gil?"

It was acknowledged and the manner of receiving relayed. By the time that part of the story had been told, both men were laughing.

"I'd give much to have seen his face when he saw you burst into the room."

"Oh, he was surprised all right. Told me later that the stupid girl should never have left a note, that he'd expressly advised her not to do so."

"Covering his tracks, eh? And heartless too. Bad enough he should abscond with my sister, but to leave my mother in ignorance is beyond cruelty."

"Well, I trust I wreaked your revenge for you, as I am confident we will not see him in London for some time to come. Ah," he said in response to a knock on the door. "Food at last. I'm famished."

They adjourned to the dining room, all of Brew's questions answered, to enjoy a quiet meal together. Quiet, that is, apart from Gil once more embarking upon all the details of his coming nuptials and his adoration of his young bride.

The following evening, the major escorted his mother and sister to a ball which was attended also by the Carstairs and Lambert families. Brew was delighted that his sister was able to walk tall, filled with admiration for her bravery in confronting a large number of people when she most certainly had not yet had time to recover from her ordeal. Gil led her to the floor, and she was not thereafter without a partner for a single dance.

Sitting beside his mother, Brew remarked that he'd had some reservations about Becca attending so large a gathering so quickly upon the heels of her failed elopement. "But I think now it's the best thing she could have done, Mama, for moping at home wouldn't have served the purpose at all," he concluded.

"She has been all contrition. I resolved not to rebuke her and I believe that it was right not to do so. She knows she has done wrong and will be forever grateful to Gil Carstairs for rescuing her from what she now realises would have been a terrible fate. Also to Harriet, for those few days at Merivale gave her the opportunity to come to terms with her situation. I truly think that is what has given her the strength to make an appearance here this evening."

"I believe she will recover sooner than we might possibly have hoped, for her pride will carry her through. Fortunately she was brought to see Fletcher in his true colours, so she will not be pining for him. She put her hand on my arm earlier, before we left the house, and though I could feel her fingers trembling, she said, 'I shall do, Brew. With such support from family and friends, how could I not?'"

"We are fortunate indeed, are we not? Tell me, if you will, when you plan to return to Austerly?" she said, changing the subject abruptly.

"I think I mustn't linger in London for too long. There is much to be done, but I see no reason why I cannot regularly travel between here and Lincolnshire. At this time of the year the roads are at their best, and I will take advantage of that. And what of you and Becca, Mama? Will you remain in the capital for long?"

The Wares had hired the house in Duke Street for the season, and Elizabeth told her son, "We will remain here in the hope that this dreadful episode will be well and truly behind us. I have not yet despaired of a match for your sister, but she will need a little time before she can move on. It is my earnest wish to see her established, and I will not be in a position to bring her back next year if I cannot turn her off this summer."

"Is there any reason other than securing the funding for such an undertaking?"

"None at all, but you must be aware of your father's circumstances."

Brew didn't know whether to smile or be angry. He chose the former and said gently, "And you know that I am full of juice and well able to provide for her. And that I would be more than happy to do so."

"If your father will allow you," his mother said doubtfully.

"It is to be hoped it won't be necessary for Becca's sake but, if it is, well, I will have plenty of time to persuade Papa that his daughter's happiness is of greater importance than his own pride."

At last she laughed and Brew was able to relax, knowing that she was reassured. Sarah and Matthew Carstairs approached a few moments later, and he left her side to go in search of Harriet. It was approaching supper time and he found her with her sister and the ever-present Gil.

"May I be permitted to escort you, Miss Lambert?"

"Oh yes," cried Amabel, "let us all go in together."

Thus Brew was able to spend some considerable time with Harriet, managing even later in the evening to sit by her during one of the few dances in which she was not engaged.

"I am aware that I have already thanked you for your services to my sister. May I say again how grateful we all are for your help and your discretion?"

Harriet turned to him and laughed, unaware how mesmerised he was by the brightness of her sparkling green eyes. "You may, sir, but only if you promise it will be the last time. What then are friends for, if not to help each other in times of trouble? I would hope my own friends would be equally ready to aid me should the need arise."

"Nothing would give me greater pleasure, Miss Lambert. I am and will always remain at your service."

Harriet looked a little shocked by his words, for they were very close to sounding like a declaration.

"I must leave again for Austerly the day after tomorrow in order to have sufficient time to return and support Gil at the wedding," Brew went on, making his intentions clearer. "I hope you will allow me the honour of calling upon you tomorrow morning before I go."

"It is always a pleasure to see you, sir," Harriet managed to reply.

Brew dressed with more than his usual care the next day. Poor François was reduced to speaking in French and at such a rate that even his fluent master was unable to follow. The cause of his distress was Brew's constant pacing and tearing from his neck several cravats which even his meticulous valet had deemed perfect. Finally, he was satisfied. A vision in black and silver enough to warm any young lady's heart, he left the house.

As he was invited by a footman into the Lambert residence in Hay Hill, Brew handed over his hat and ran his fingers through the ever recalcitrant shock of blond hair. As always it fell back over his forehead. He had hoped to find Harriet alone, but both her mother and her sister were with her when he entered the drawing room. Containing his patience and nerves as best he could, he engaged them in polite conversation for some minutes, enquiring of Amabel if all was in train for her forthcoming wedding. She knew him well enough now not to be bashful in his company, and he therefore received more information than perhaps he had expected as she spoke at length of the arrangements that had been put in place. He accepted also the refreshment that was offered, and it was consequently some time later that he was at last able to say, "Miss Lambert, it is such a fine day, I wonder if you would do me the favour of taking a turn with me about the garden."

Harriet acquiesced and had it not been for the hint of a sparkle in her expressive green eyes, his courage might have deserted him, for he truly had no idea how his proposal would be received. She was certainly not short of admirers and he had observed her many times enjoying the company of other men, doing something he was unable to, such as dancing. And now, as he stood back to allow her to pass before him onto the terrace, he had to lay his heart before her.

Harriet was outwardly calm as she preceded Brew into the garden. It was a beautiful spring day — warm, even, as summer was approaching. They took a turn about the paths before sitting on the same bench as they had on the night of Amabel's ball. Though Harriet had some strange sensation in her stomach, she turned to face him. She prayed he would say what she was hoping to hear, but whatever the next few minutes brought she would meet it head on. He seemed somewhat at a loss for words, so she filled the gap that threatened to become uncomfortable.

"I trust your trip to Austerly tomorrow is not due to some problem? Your father is well, I hope?"

It relieved the tension and she was grateful to see a rueful smile, something that transformed him immediately, for nothing was more certain than that the major was not his usual urbane self. His hand went once more to his hair before it moved, seemingly of its own volition, to take one of hers.

"My father is well, thank you, and I must tell you I left him in good heart. Miss Lambert, Harriet, you cannot by now be in any doubt as to my feelings towards you." Her hand quivered in his but remained where it was. "In almost no time after our first meeting, I fell deeply in love with you."

Harriet remained still and waited for him to continue, but she smiled in what she hoped was an encouraging way.

"It has for some while now been my earnest wish that you become my wife. I know I come to you damaged…"

"I beg your pardon?" Harriet interrupted. "I don't understand. Is there something you haven't told me, something that has occurred in your past?"

"No, I believe I have confided in you everything of any significance."

"Then what on earth do you mean by damaged?"

"You must know. My leg. I am no longer a whole man."

Harriet rose abruptly to her feet and strode up and down. He too stood up and looked on, bewildered by her reaction. Eventually she came to a halt in front of him, but the anger on her face was clear to see. "How dare you!" she spat at him.

"I do dare. It is the truth, after all, and nothing can change that," he said, his own anger matching hers.

"Then you are a fool, Major Ware. You, who have fought for your country, should know that the value of a man is not in his physical abilities but in his courage and strength of character. Not only are you a fool, but you should also be ashamed. Many men were wounded to a far greater extent than you have been.

Even more lost their lives. So don't you talk to me about being damaged, because I will not have it!" she said, stamping her foot. She paused, her anger spent, but so too was his.

Brew put his finger under her chin and raised it so that she might look directly at him once more. "Harriet, my darling girl, don't be enraged with me. I offer you my hand and my heart and if I am less than perfect, well, I offer you that too. I meant no disrespect to those brave men of whom you speak. Marry me and you will make me the happiest man on earth."

Tears sparkled on the ends of her lashes but she smiled through them and, as he bent to kiss her, she raised her lips to his. As they stepped back from each other, Harriet lifted her hand to brush the hair from his face. "I am so sorry you are to go away tomorrow, but I can be comforted now in the knowledge that when you return we can be together always." She smiled, a mischievous look making him wonder what she would say next. "And may we now go and tell my mother? She will be *so* delighted."

CHAPTER NINETEEN

Words were unnecessary, for Harriet and Brew had entered the drawing room hand in hand. Louisa jumped to her feet and Amabel ran to embrace her sister. Gil, who had arrived in their absence, shook his friend's hand warmly and thumped him on the shoulder, nearly knocking him off balance in his enthusiasm.

"So now we are to be brothers-in-law, eh, Brew? I shouldn't have liked it at all if Harriet had married that popinjay — what's 'is name? You know, the one with the striped waistcoats."

Harriet laughed but scolded him all the same. "He is merely unsure of himself and dresses so to hide it."

"He does? Well, I'll be damned — beg your pardon, dashed. Still prefer Brew, though."

"Well, so do I, as it happens, which is just as well. It must of course have been my earnest wish to marry to suit your pleasure."

"You asked for that, old boy," Brew said with a laugh before accepting a salute on the cheek from Louisa, who expressed her approval at her daughter's choice.

"I cannot believe I am to have two daughters wed in the same year. When do you plan to be married?"

"We have had no time to discuss details as yet. I am still basking in the joy of Harriet's acceptance and have not thought beyond that."

"Well, it is not much over a week until Amabel and Gil's wedding, so we must get that out of the way first."

"Mama!" cried her offended child.

"Now then, Amabel, you know very well I didn't mean it like that. Merely that to be considering at the same time two events of such magnitude is more than your poor mother can cope with."

Amabel hugged Louisa and apologised while assuring her that she had only been funning.

Harriet had spoken barely a word but, seated now beside Brew, she looked more serene than he had ever seen her. "I hope you don't mind waiting just a little while," she whispered to him.

He took her hand and pressed her fingers to his lips. "Of course I'm impatient, but it's barely an hour since I could believe that you had accepted me. I would not wish to encroach on the happiness of these two. Our time will come. With your permission, I will send a notice to the *Morning Post* upon my return. You will understand that I do not want to be away from you when our situation is made known. I would wish to be beside you so we may receive the congratulations of our friends together."

She was grateful for his thoughtfulness and hoped he would return to London very soon.

Brew rose a short while later and excused himself. "I must tell my mother and my sister, for I will not have time to pay them a visit before I leave in the morning. I have much to do, so I shall not see you again today. Take care while I am away, my darling. The hours cannot fly quickly enough until we are together again."

After Brew's departure, Harriet excused herself and went to her room. She had been surprised to see this romantic side of Brew, something she had never had a hint of before. Once or twice, perhaps, she had observed a look or a gesture which she'd hoped was indicative of more than mere friendship, but she was charmed by his ability to express himself in such a way. She wanted an hour or two alone to reflect upon all that had happened and to daydream about their future together.

Brew chose to ride into Lincolnshire, judging it would be quicker and not on this occasion needing his carriage, though another followed with François and his luggage. As a soldier, even as an officer, he had been accustomed to taking care of his own attire when necessary, but on this visit he intended to engage with some of his neighbours and wished to be suitably turned out. Definitely his wardrobe and his valet needed to be on hand. The Carstairs family were fixed in London, but there were others to whom he wished to pay his respects. As he rode, he reflected upon his conversation with his mother and Rebecca the previous day.

"You have made me very happy, Brew. I have no doubt your father too will be pleased, for even he has remarked on a certain presence that Miss Lambert has about her," Elizabeth had said.

"And Harriet has been so good to me, I couldn't be more pleased that she will be my sister," Rebecca had added.

Brew had really had no qualms about their approval of his choice of bride. He hoped his mother was right and that the squire would be similarly in favour of the match. It was his wish that Harriet would consent to reside in Lincolnshire, for he had much work to do there even while his father was yet the incumbent at Austerly. Though he would not ask her to live in the house, it would be likely that they would see much of each other. One of the reasons now added to all the rest for going home was to investigate what properties might be suitable. Next time he made this journey, he intended to take Harriet with him so that she might inspect those he had chosen for her to see. More content than he could ever remember being, Brew was at peace as he travelled into his home county.

Harriet passed the time as best she could during Brew's absence. There was much to be done still for the wedding of Amabel to Gil; with only a few days remaining, there were adjustments to be made to gowns, accessories to be finalised and a number of morning calls to be made and received. Nevertheless, she found time to ride Brandy every day. With only her groom for company, she enjoyed the solitude that permitted her freedom to contemplate her own position, something it was impossible to do at home where all was at present focused upon her sister.

Basking in the sunshine of her happiness, Harriet could not but be curious as to what plans if any her affianced husband had in mind for their future. They'd had no time at all to discuss the prospect broadly, let alone talk over any of the finer details. And so she schemed in her head, wondering above all how soon their own nuptials could take place. Merivale was so close to her heart that even thinking about leaving her childhood home brought a lump to her throat. Harriet hoped she and Brew might pay regular visits, infrequent though they might have to be, for she had no doubt they must reside close to his home in Lincolnshire, and the distance between there and Kent was not inconsiderable.

What troubled her most of all was her mother's situation. Louisa was not long widowed, and soon neither of her daughters would be living with her. Mama was an independent woman who was more inclined to go out every day than to remain at home sewing or reading. Moreover, Harriet knew her mother didn't have the love for Merivale that she herself had inherited from her father. It was a big house in a somewhat isolated area. *Well*, she told herself, *there is little if anything I can do to resolve that problem*, which thought had provoked an involuntary pressure on Brandy's sides from his mistress and caused him to step out. She reined him back in and patted his neck, for the error had been hers. Determined not to fret over what she could not control, she gave herself up to the enjoyment of her ride.

On two occasions she found time to visit Duke Street knowing that, in spite of her bravery, there could be little doubt the next weeks were going to be difficult for Rebecca Ware. When Elizabeth left the two young women together, she admitted as much.

"I spoke only the truth when I told you how lucky I am to be rid of such a man, but oh, Harriet, for a while I loved him so much. It's hard to let those feelings go, even knowing they were misplaced."

"And no-one who knows you and loves you would expect an immediate recovery. Not only were you deceived, but you were frightened as well. I swear, if Gil hadn't planted Fletcher a facer I should have done so myself!"

This made Becca laugh. It was a step. A small one, and she still had a long way to go, but there was no way she was going to allow the experience to define her. Turning the subject, she said, "I can't believe you allowed my brother to run away at such a time. Did you truly not discuss your plans at all?"

Harriet returned her smile, though with a certain resignation. "In this instance I cannot allow you to blame him. His plans were already in place when he made his offer, and he could not delay his departure or else he would miss the wedding. He is to stand as groomsman for Gil, you know, and being absent would be unforgivable."

"But no announcement of your own engagement has been made."

"With good reason: it is our wish that we receive felicitations from our friends together. Imagine, Becca, how I might have felt if the news were known and I alone were here to be congratulated. No, thus far your brother has done everything right. My hope is that your father will receive the disclosure with good will, for I would hate anything to throw a rub in the way of their reconciliation."

Harriet need not have worried about Cornelius Ware's reaction to the news that his son was to be married. There was no denying the frailty of his body, but his spirit seemed to have regained its vigour and he and Brew were every day closer to reaching an understanding. Nobody could have been more surprised than the major when his father invited him for a day's fishing.

"It is a sport I enjoyed as a young man but have not indulged in of late. Would you care to join me?"

"I should be delighted, sir. We have a meeting with Pullman this afternoon, but the weather looks fair for tomorrow. Would that suit you?"

"It would. And talking of Pullman, he speaks highly of you, boy. Tells me you're a fast learner."

This was said with so much goodwill that Brew could scarcely believe his ears but made haste to assure him that it was as much his father's instruction as that of the steward that was proving so helpful. He could have said nothing better, and though the squire brushed the words aside it was evident that he was much pleased with his son, and never more so than when his advice was sought as to a suitable establishment for the future Major and Mrs Ware.

"You could do worse than Old Lofty's place," Cornelius said, laughing at the memory of a now deceased old friend who'd stood taller than any of his acquaintance. "Or Winthrop's house. There are no heirs to inherit the property and his widow has married again. At her age! I could scarce believe it when I heard!" He chuckled again, and Brew was grateful both for the guidance and the lifting of his father's mood.

He knew he would have to raise the subject of the wishing well before long but decided to leave it until after they'd been fishing. He was mindful of his mother's request and would leave it in place, but more extensive work had to be done to it before he could be satisfied. He also had the intention of engraving something in Nancy's memory, but it was best not to raise the matter until he had to.

With so much to do in a few short days, Brew appreciated taking time out with his father to go fishing, little though he could spare it. In the end they spent only half a day, Cornelius saying it was more than enough time to be sitting still in one place, but there was something approaching empathy between the two men.

Returning to the house, the major called for his horse and went to visit one of the properties the squire had recommended, there still being more than sufficient daylight for him to get back before dark. He found it suited him very well and hoped Harriet would feel the same, though he hadn't discounted 'Old Lofty's' place, which he had yet to see. It would be for his bride to decide. Riding back in the direction of the setting sun, his thoughts were on the day after tomorrow, when he would be returning to London. His father had asked that he convey his apologies to the Lamberts and the

Carstairs family, as he would not be attending the wedding, feeling unable to face the journey so soon after his last trip to town. Brew suspected that it was as much a lack of desire as a want of ability but did not say so.

All things considered, his trip had gone well. The squire had placed little in the way of his suggestions for Austerly, other than occasionally to impose his will, more for the sake of it than with good reason. It was quite evident that he took pleasure in at last seeing the transformation of his run-down inheritance into a modern residence with every facility and comfort. It would not all happen at once, of course, but he could divine from the plans how it might all end up. Brew had to give him credit also for being just as interested in the estate as he was in Austerly itself. He hoped they would part on better terms than they had previously enjoyed, but sadly it was not to be the case.

Rather apprehensively at dinner the next evening, he brought up the matter of the wishing well. "Though it had been my intention to raze it to the ground, it is my mother's wish that it remains. It seems these days she draws comfort from it when looking through the window."

"Your intention? You upstart! Who do you think you are, changing everything to your own desire?" Cornelius snapped.

Obviously he had touched a nerve. Brew smiled at his sire's perversity. "But you have yourself wished to leave it there all these years, sir. Why do you now object that it should continue to be so?"

"You come back here, throwing your weight around, thinking you have the right to alter things as you wish!" his father blustered.

Brew attempted to mollify him, but it seemed things had gone beyond that.

"If I wish to pull it down, I shall do so!" Cornelius shouted, his face now red with rage. He faced only calmness from his son.

"With no thought as to my mother's sentiments?" he asked in a quiet but steely voice.

"What does she know about it?" Cornelius replied, now being pushed into a corner and with nowhere to go.

"That is as callous and hurtful as anything you have said. She, who must look at it every day as she sits in her drawing room, is surely in a better position than anyone to have a considered opinion on the matter. And even if she didn't, do her feelings not hold any sway with you?" Brew paused for a moment before leaving his father in no doubt as to his intentions. "If in my absence you should remove the well, I shall withhold all funding for the further improvement of the property until such time as it becomes mine. Do I make myself understood?"

The squire had never seen this side of his son. Not for nothing had Brew risen to the rank of major. In the habit of being in command, there was no way he would allow his father to ride roughshod over him, certainly not where his mother's welfare was concerned. Cornelius left the room without another word, slamming the door behind him as he went. By the time Brew left the next morning, they had neither spoken to nor seen each other again.

CHAPTER TWENTY

There were only two days until the wedding and the excitement in Hay Hill was tangible. Brew had written to Harriet from Lincolnshire reassuring her that things were progressing well, especially with his father, something which warmed her heart. She could only speculate as to the hurt that lay between the two men, and the knowledge that they were once again on terms after so many years was encouraging.

Resisting the temptation to keep rushing to the window in anticipation of his arrival, for she knew he would return some time that day, Harriet sat with her mother in the drawing room, as composed as she could possibly be under the circumstances. Amabel was out walking with Gil and, expecting their return, she hardly glanced up when the door opened but quickly jumped to her feet when she saw that it was Brew who had entered the room. Louisa, having greeted her prospective son-in-law, left them alone together.

"No doubt you have much to discuss," she said as she left.

The couple embraced before Brew led Harriet to the couch and sat down beside her. He did not release her hands.

"What a splendid woman your mother is. It is considerate of her to leave us alone."

"I may once or twice have mentioned that I'm keen to speak with you," Harriet replied with a very saucy smile. "But tell me first, your trip went well? I was delighted to learn that you and the squire are getting on so famously."

A frown marred Brew's features and she looked at him anxiously. "And that was the case until the evening before I left. I brought up the subject of the wishing well and my mother's desire that it should remain in place. Perversely my father, who has all these years refused to have it removed, decided it was an unreasonable request. He fired off at me in such a rage as to raise my concern for his health. I feared apoplexy. He stormed out of the room, and I did not speak to him again before my departure."

"Do you think he is unwell, then?"

"Only in temper," Brew laughed. "I must tell you, though, that in spite of everything I owe him my thanks. He was in a position to recommend to me two properties which might prove suitable for us as a home after we are married. Both are eminently so, though I did like one above the other. I am hoping you will not object to living in proximity to Austerly, as it will make things far easier to oversee than were we to live in the south."

Harriet raised her hand to his cheek. "If I cannot live at Merivale, I care not where I am, only that I am with you."

Brew naturally demonstrated his approval of her sacrifice before adding, "It is my intention now to place an advertisement of our betrothal in the *Morning Post*, and I wanted to discuss the wording with you before doing so."

She glanced at the paper he pulled out. "I can see nothing amiss at all but I would ask, if you do not object, that we wait until after the wedding. So close as it is, I would not wish to draw any attention away from Amabel and Gil. I'm sure you understand."

"I do and I honour your sentiments, though I must tell you, my darling, that I am becoming very impatient to call you my own."

This declaration of his love naturally called for another embrace. They sprang apart guiltily when the door opened and

Louisa entered, accompanied by the young couple. Everyone laughed and the two men shook hands heartily.

"I am at your service, Gil. Is there anything you wish me to do for you?"

"No more than support me at the ceremony, for I fear my legs may give way beneath me."

"Are you truly nervous?" Amabel asked.

"Not at all, my sweet. Truthfully it cannot come soon enough for me."

And so it was that four contented young people sat down to enjoy the tea for which Louisa had rung.

The threatened rain did not materialise, and the sun shone brightly when Miss Amabel Lambert was joined in matrimony to the Honourable Gilbert Sebastian Carstairs. The groom, though usually flamboyantly attired, chose on this morning to tone down his clothing. As he confided to the major, "It's Amabel's day. I wouldn't want to take the shine out of her in any way, so I decided to keep it simple for a change."

Brew approved of his decision, admiring the dove-grey pantaloons and embroidered waistcoat of the same colour. He was himself immaculate as ever in black and silver. "I am happy to see you have not fallen into the trap of attempting anything outrageous with your cravat. This economy of style suits you, I must say, and I like the cut of your coat. Your tailor has done a fine job."

Gil fingered the lapel of his dark blue tailcoat with satisfaction, happy to have attained his friend's approval. There was an element of discomposure in the action too, nervous as he was standing in St George's with Brew while waiting for his bride. All tension disappeared as she approached him on the arm of Matthew Carstairs who, standing in loco parentis, escorted her to his son's side. Amabel had chosen a dress of fine white muslin over which she wore a soft silk shawl shot with a pale canary hue that complemented her own yellow curls. These were only partially obscured by a small cap trimmed with lace purchased in the most delightful emporium which she had visited one day with Lady Sawcroft.

Gil drew in his breath in admiration of her beauty and stood proudly as the ancient ritual took place, whereupon they received the congratulations of their companions. The whole party then adjourned to Brook Street, where the groom's parents had arranged a wedding breakfast. Present at this function were the families of the happy couple, the Wares (minus the squire) and old Lady Sawcroft, together with a dozen or so intimate friends. Amabel and Gil were to remain in town until the following day, so Sarah Carstairs had taken the opportunity to extend the celebration by engaging musicians so that dancing might take place. Harriet was astonished when Brew approached her and begged the honour of standing up with her.

"But … your leg…" she whispered.

"…is much improved to the extent that I am able to manage without a walking aid." Brew smiled, and it reached her heart. "I have been following my doctor's instructions and undertaking a variety of exercises which have improved matters no end. To be truthful, I have been disguising my progress from you by continuing to employ the stick, for I wanted it to be a surprise."

"You have certainly succeeded in that regard," she said, eyes wide open.

"Then join me, if you will. The next set is forming. I hope I don't disgrace you."

"You could never do that, Brew, and you must promise to tell me if you need to withdraw."

She rose to her feet and they astonished everyone present by joining the rest of the dancers. Brew acquitted himself well, to his immense relief. Though he had practised the steps in the privacy of his own home, he had experienced a certain trepidation, knowing it would be an entirely different experience in company and with a partner. By the time the set was finished, he was somewhat pulled but exhilarated. He accepted both Harriet's praise for his accomplishment and her command that he do no more that day.

Lady Sawcroft, who happened to be passing and observed all, rapped him on the knuckles and accused him of hiding his light under a bushel. "Now I shall be expecting you stand up with me on another occasion, young man," she exclaimed. "Very prettily done. Yes, very pretty." With that she moved on, chuckling gleefully.

Brew appeared on the steps of the house in Hay Hill the next day before the morning was much advanced. He found Harriet on the point of going for a walk with her mama down to and around Berkeley Square.

"May I be permitted then to escort you both, or would you perhaps prefer to be alone?"

Harriet informed him that she and Louisa had had ample time to discuss yesterday's events, though they would doubtless continue to do so for some time to come. "After all," she said, laughing as Brew fell into step beside them, "there has been insufficient opportunity to express our opinion on every gown and hair arrangement, the gossip about this one and that, and the refreshments that were provided."

"My sister-in-law was in fine form, was she not?" Louisa added. "She told me she hadn't enjoyed herself as much for years and that she is determined you shall take to the floor with her at the very next opportunity."

"Then I must find some immediate reason to take me out of town, Mrs Lambert, for the woman terrifies me!" Brew jested.

They met no-one of their acquaintance during their outing, and when they returned to the house Louisa once more excused herself.

"I've said it before and I'll…" Brew began.

"Yes, she is a treasure to be sure. And she's right, of course. There is much we need to discuss," said Harriet.

She looked a little grave but Brew did not question her. He simply said, "It was a disappointment that we encountered none of our friends while we were out. The announcement of our betrothal has appeared in this morning's *Post*, and if you must know I am as proud as a peacock and expect jealous comments from all."

"Then I am certain you will be sorely disappointed, sir. I am not so vain," Harriet threw back at him while at the same time softening the blow by placing a hand on his shoulder and looking adoringly into his eyes. A mistake, for conversation ceased to flow for several moments.

Brew put her away from him once more and said sternly, "This will not do. Tell me, if you will, how soon I may take you to Lincolnshire so that you may inspect the two houses I mentioned."

The grave look returned, and this time he did enquire as to the cause.

"It is Mama."

"Is there something amiss?" he asked, truly concerned.

"Not as such. It's just, well, please let us sit down and I will try to make you understand." She grasped his hands, something that was fast becoming a comfortable habit with her. "Mama is the best, most generous and compassionate person, and what I am about to say must not reach her ears. I appreciate the necessity of securing our future home, but I am reluctant to leave her alone so soon after my sister's wedding. I fear it will take her a while to become accustomed to being on her own, and it is my fervent wish that I do all I can to ease the way for her."

Brew could see where this was going, and while it wasn't what he wished he could value Harriet's sentiments.

"I'm happy for us to proceed with arrangements for our own wedding…" she began.

"You'd better be," he interrupted, pretending to be grim but with a smile which gave him away.

"Only I feel I cannot leave her quite yet," Harriet continued. "If you must go to Austerly, I will rely on your good judgement to decide what is best for us." She looked at him appealingly.

"Naturally it is not what I would wish but I think I must go back, not just to secure a home for us but because I left my father in bad frame. I could never forgive myself if he were to fall ill on account of our quarrel."

As much as he understood her predicament, so did she understand his. They decided to delay their plans until he returned again to London. In the meantime, they would call the banns which would give them a three-month period in which to marry.

"When do you go, Brew?"

"I will visit my mother and sister tomorrow but will leave London the day after. I can only be grateful for your compassion. You must know I will return as soon as I may. Can I persuade you to ride with me once more this afternoon?"

"I should like nothing more, my dearest."

And so once more the two were parted, Harriet to do what she might to help her mother establish a new kind of life in the future and Brew with the more worrying task of once more bridging the gap between himself and his father. He wasn't at all sure it could be done. He was relieved when he reached Austerly to find that the squire had not, in a fit of pique, torn down the wishing well. Brew arrived on the steps of the house just as the door was opened and Pullman was taking his leave of Cornelius. To Brew's relief, his father acknowledged him, though the steward was obviously aware of the sometime animosity between the two men.

"Good day, Major," said Pullman. "The squire and I have just been discussing some of the aspects that you and I talked about on your last visit. He has suggested one or two minor adjustments, but nothing that will substantially alter what we planned, isn't that so, Squire Ware?"

Cornelius grunted agreement, mumbled good day and turned on his heel.

Shaking hands with the steward, Brew said anxiously, "I trust things are proceeding for the most part along the lines we agreed?"

"Oh yes, never you worry, sir. Your father has been in the saddle for so long, I would not wish to appear in any way to flout his authority, but he's a reasonable man."

Brew raised an astonished eyebrow. "He is?"

"Yes, but you must understand his position. Your wishes will all be adhered to, but I see no necessity for, ahem, ruffling the old master's feathers. And it would be unkind to do so."

Brew took the point and, as he wished the man good day, he entered the house far readier for appeasement than argument. He found Cornelius in the library.

"I did not look to see you again so soon, boy," he snapped. "Is young Carstairs now safely married?"

"He is, sir, and he asked me to convey his regret that you were unable to attend the wedding." This wasn't true, but it couldn't hurt his father to think so. "And I came as soon as I could, because I couldn't bear that we had once more parted on bad terms, you and I." He sat down, and both his face and voice softened. "I am your son, am I not? Nothing is more certain than that I have inherited several of your traits, both good and bad." He chuckled. "I make no doubt that had I remained at Austerly, we would many times have been at loggerheads. That does not mean I do not hold you in the highest respect."

Brew sat back and folded one leg over the other, looking down at his splattered boots and trusting that François would not be far behind him. As he glanced up again, he was relieved to see a softening of his father's shoulders and a reluctant acknowledgement of the comparison between them.

"No doubt you cajoled your men in just such a way, Brew."

"Not at all, sir. Merely I would not ask them to go where I could not lead. Each would have died for me and I for them. In fact — and this is something I have shared with no-one before today — just such a thing occurred when I sustained the injury to my leg. I am fortunate to be here today. One of my soldiers lies buried in France because he flung me out of the way. I was wounded, yes, but he … well, it is something I have had to learn to live with. War is not a pretty thing."

Cornelius looked at Brew as though he had never seen him before. Wonder, pride, sadness — all these emotions vied for supremacy, but it was pride that won. He stood and moved around the table to stand next to his son. "I should like to shake your hand."

Brew rose to his feet. "And I yours, sir." They stood thus for a moment or two before the younger grinned and said, "And now you will please excuse me, for I am covered with dirt and would change my clothes. I should consider it an honour if you would join me for dinner, Papa, in say an hour? I am absolutely famished. Do you still have some of that good quality burgundy laid up? I must say, that too would go down a treat."

He left the room and ran up the staircase. His leg had improved so much that he scarcely watched his step. As he went, he reflected that nothing was more certain than that in the future he and his father would be at outs many times, but that a seemingly insurmountable barrier had at last been removed.

CHAPTER TWENTY-ONE

Harriet was missing Brew. With Amabel and Gil away on their honeymoon, a further gap was left in her day-to-day existence. Shrugging off the threatening ennui, she spent time every morning with Brandy, her daily ride a source of solace and enjoyment all at once. For the rest, she and Louisa were never at a loss. The knocker in Hay Hill was rarely still and, when they weren't entertaining visitors, time was spent shopping, attending suppers and soirées and enjoying the pleasure of the lengthening days. On occasion both could be found reading in the garden in companionable silence, a welcome respite from a very busy life. But still she longed for Brew.

"Did I tell you, Harriet, that Matilda is to visit us this afternoon?"

"I don't recall that you did, but it's always a pleasure to see her these days. Like Brew, she terrifies me, or she did before I came to know her better. I believe I am no longer frowned upon as I was when a child, and I have discovered that beneath the brusqueness lies a kind heart."

Louisa patted her daughter's knee. "Allow me to reassure you, dearest. She told me herself that she would not have believed you would develop into such an amiable young woman."

Moments later Lady Sawcroft was shown in, and Harriet and her mother were hard put to find a reason to put forward as to why both were reduced to a fit of giggling.

"Well, I dare say I shouldn't find it amusing. You are like a pair of children in the schoolroom. Now, I've come to ask you, Louisa, if you would care to visit me at Sawcroft House at the end of the season. I plan to return there when it becomes too hot and stuffy to remain in town, and I would count it a favour if you would join me. Harriet will by then have married her major, I assume," she said, looking enquiringly at her niece.

"Nothing is fixed yet, Aunt Matilda. I am awaiting Brew's return from Austerly. Until then, like you I can only speculate." She said no more, entirely unsure as to whether or not the invitation was welcome to her mother.

"What a delightful idea," Louisa said, surprising Harriet a little. "It is kind of you to invite me, Matilda."

Lady Sawcroft did not remain long, telling them she needed to return home to change as she was that evening going to the theatre with Mr and Mrs Carstairs.

"I do not know why I bother to retain a box because I so rarely go, but Sarah expressed a wish to see the play before they return to Langborne."

"Are they to go soon, then? I did not know."

"Nor I, Harriet, and I believe not yet, but it is a good opportunity, they and I being free. Perhaps you would like to join us. I understand you have established quite a friendship with them."

Louisa accepted the invitation, but Harriet had planned to write to Brew that evening and declined so graciously as to win her aunt's approval once more. When she had gone, mother and daughter grinned at one another.

"No, Mama, it is unkind of us to make game of her but I must say, when she walked in I didn't know where to put myself."

"Nor I. And then she was so kind."

"Would you indeed like to visit her at Sawcroft House?"

"Oh yes, my dear. Matilda and I are much more tolerant of each other than we were used to be. I have become quite fond of her, in fact, and I enjoy her caustic tongue, for she is never malicious."

"In that case, I am delighted for you. Now, will you just look at the hour! If you are to join her and Mr and Mrs Carstairs this evening, it is time you changed into something more suitable."

A while later Harriet waved her mother off then went to the library to pen a note to her fiancé and to sit for a while, pondering her future. It was a pleasant occupation, and her letter was only half-written when she heard a disturbance outside. Alarmed, she pushed back her chair and ran into the hall. She was shocked to see Arthur, filthy, dishevelled and obviously in considerable distress.

"Miss Lambert, I came as quickly as I could. Mr Butterfield sent me, he did, him needing to remain at Merivale and deal with things, which I couldn't, no, nor Ben neither."

"What has happened, Arthur? In plain words, if you will, and quickly."

"There's been a fire. Half the house is gone, miss, and them still trying to put out the flames when I left. Mr Butterfield thought as how you'd want to know as soon as possible!"

Harriet felt her knees grow weak and she clasped the doorframe for support. For a moment her mind went blank, before her natural competence rose to the forefront. "Have Brandy saddled up and brought round. We will leave for Merivale immediately."

"But miss, we couldn't possibly, not at this time of night."

"No, you're right, Arthur. Where have my wits gone a-begging? You must get some rest now, for I wish to leave at first light. But I will take Brandy. Riding will be faster. But whatever am I thinking? Tell me at once. Has anyone been hurt?"

Arthur shuffled his feet before taking a deep breath. When he spoke, there was a shudder in his voice. "Mary, the kitchen maid, was badly burned, Miss Lambert. Her cries were that awful to listen to. And we lost Evie, what had just had a new litter. The kittens also."

Harriet was on the point of questioning him further when she realised the poor man must be exhausted. "If there are no further casualties, let us continue this tomorrow, Arthur. In the meantime, have something to eat and get a good night's sleep. I shall see you in the morning."

Leaving the footman to deal with the young groom, Harriet retreated into the library and sank once again onto the chair she had earlier occupied. The half-finished letter was lying there, so she picked up her pen and began to convey what had occurred:

Naturally I will know more when I am in Kent, but you will see that I must go. You know what Merivale means to me. Mama is due home from the theatre shortly and I dread telling her what has happened, but I shall insist that she remain in London. Nothing can be gained by the two of us going, and I would save her distress if I can.

Arthur tells me that one of the maids is badly injured but made no mention of any others aside from the house cat and her litter of kittens. I pray nothing has befallen anyone else and am anxious to get home as quickly as I can to see what damage has been sustained. My head is reeling, my love, and I cannot think clearly. Be assured I shall write to you again as soon as I may. I know we looked to see each other in London next week, but if things are even half as bad as my groom has intimated I shall be fixed in Kent for some time.

Please give my respects to your father and tell him, well, you will know what to say.

Harriet

She had just folded the paper when her mother returned home. Hearing her arrival, Harriet went once more into the hall with as much energy as she could muster. She would have an argument on her hands, she knew that, and invited Louisa to join her in the library, it being the closest room. The colour faded from her mother's face. She knew her daughter well enough to realise that something was gravely amiss.

"Sit down, Mama. I fear I have bad news."

Louisa gasped and raised her hand to her throat. "Amabel!"

"No, Mama, I have no news of Amabel and Gil, but I am certain they are well. It is Merivale. Arthur arrived while you were out. There has been a fire."

She continued to relate everything she had been told and informed Louisa of her intentions.

"But I must come with you. Let me just ring for my abigail, and she can pack what I need if nothing can be salvaged at home."

"No, think, Mama. I will be swifter if I ride. Arthur will be all the protection I need. With respect, I doubt there would be much you could do. I only pray there will be something that can be accomplished, but I am more familiar than you with the running of the place. The most recent information is that the fire had not been extinguished. It may by now have engulfed the whole house."

Louisa began to weep silently.

Harriet continued, "We should not yet despair. Until we know more, I would beg you to remain in Hay Hill. I will send a courier to you as soon as I have news. And now we must both retire. It has been a long day and I must make an early start."

They went upstairs together and Harriet attempted to divert her mother by asking about the play she had seen, but it was two very subdued women who parted company on the landing and went each to her own bedchamber.

Harriet was gone before Louisa had left her room the next day. She tried to glean more information from Arthur during those periods when they slowed to a trot to spare their horses. There was little more he could tell her, and she had to wait impatiently until they reached their destination. Allowing for necessary stops, as she did not want to change mounts, they rode onto the Merivale estate in the late afternoon. Though Harriet had for some distance been peering ahead to catch a glimpse of flames, should the fire still be raging, no evidence could be seen until they turned a bend in the drive. She swallowed hard and remarked to her groom that at least the fire appeared to have been extinguished.

"But my heart breaks to see my home in such a state," she went on. "At least the house remains standing. I feared to see it burned to the ground."

"Yes, miss, I'm fair dumbfounded to see it still there," Arthur replied gloomily.

It was fortunate that in spite of her misgivings, Harriet had been able to maintain an even temperament during the ride, for her companion's despondency had been such that she might well have expected the worst. It was thus with no little relief that she dismounted in front of the still erect pillars and sent up a prayer of thanks that the house was made of stone.

Mrs Sweet came rushing out of the house, holding her pinafore up to her eyes, whether from the smoke or as a result of her tears Harriet could not immediately discern. "Oh, Miss Lambert, such a terrible thing to happen! We are all at sixes and sevens to be sure."

"And we are all so grateful that you have coped with none of the family being at home," Harriet replied. "Tell me first, how is Mary, and have there been any other injuries?"

"You must know that Mary is not one to complain, miss, but it fair tugged at my heartstrings to see her in such a state. We've had the doctor in and though she will be scarred, poor dear, he seems confident she'll survive. It's a miracle no-one else was hurt, if you ask me."

"Then I will take Brandy to the stables myself, for he has worked hard this day and will be unfamiliar with his surroundings. Be ready afterwards to take me to Mary's room. I would like to see for myself how she is progressing."

Harriet walked Brandy to the stable block, to which Arthur had preceded her. Ben was waiting to take the horse from her and could not help but comment on the gelding's fine points. "There is a vacant stall next to Rhapsody's, as well you know. Let's hope they will be comfortable side by side. You've no need to wait, miss. I can see to him now."

But wait she did, though not for long. She could not leave without seeing Rhapsody. Standing in the mare's stall with her cheek against her neck, for a few moments she drew comfort before returning to the house and the onslaught she knew was to come.

As she entered through the front door, Harriet thought she might have imagined the whole thing. All was intact in the large entrance hall. With its marble floor and pillars, the theme having been continued inside, there was nothing to see of the catastrophe and it seemed the fire must have been contained before ever reaching this part. The pungent smell of smoke was sufficient, though, to tell her that she had not been dreaming. She went straight to see Mary, with Mrs Sweet talking all the way and filling her in on the available information as Arthur had not been able to do.

"It's just the west wing that's been damaged, Miss Lambert, though heaven knows that's bad enough. Struck by lightning, we were. A storm that came out of nowhere. One minute the sky was as blue as could be, then all of a sudden these black clouds came sweeping across and we could hear the thunder rumbling. Like night, it was, until the lightning lit up the sky like a giant firework. Eerie, it was. And then it was gone, but poor Mary was in the pantry and got caught in the flames. Well, here we are. I daresay you might like to ask her yourself, but the doctor said to keep her as quiet as possible. Anyone but you and I wouldn't let them in."

Mrs Sweet, having exhausted herself with her account, opened the door and Harriet stepped inside. There was a sense of stillness in the attic room and for a moment she feared the worst, but as she moved towards the bed she could see the gentle movement of the girl's chest as she breathed. Lucy, the chambermaid, was seated next to her, looking almost as pale as the bandages in which Mary was swathed. She stood up and moved away and Harriet took her place.

Taking the girl's hand, though only the fingertips were visible, she talked gently to her, expressing her sorrow at what had happened and her admiration for the maid's bravery. There was no response and Harriet couldn't be sure she'd been heard. Aware that there was nothing she could do, she gave way to Lucy and left the room to inspect the damage. It was growing dark now and she couldn't see much in the way of detail, but it was obvious even at a cursory glance that the west wing would need rebuilding entirely.

Mrs Sweet sought her out and told her firmly to go straight to the dining room. "We have a portable stove set up on the other side of the house and Cook has rustled up something for you, so you mustn't disappoint her, must you?"

It was as if she were a child again, the old retainer adopting the same tone she had used with the younger Harriet when she had grazed her knee or taken a tumble from her horse. At once she realised both how tired and how hungry she was. "Thank you, Mrs Sweet. You are right, that would never do."

She went gratefully as instructed, made a hearty meal and fell exhausted into bed not long after. Whatever the damage, it would wait until tomorrow.

CHAPTER TWENTY-TWO

Brew had just signed the lease on the Winthrop property when he received Harriet's letter. His first instinct was to fly immediately to her side, and he glanced at the French mantel clock in the library before saying to Pullman, "Thank you, I believe that's all. I am grateful for your assistance in this matter, as with everything else. Our plans for Austerly are progressing well, and it seems I must again journey south." He waved the correspondence in the air and, though he did not make the steward aware of its contents, he added, "Something has occurred which may delay my plans. I shall know more in due course. In the meantime, I would be grateful if you would continue to oversee things here. Good day, Mr Pullman." The two shook hands and, alone once more, Brew reread the letter.

He picked up a pen to reply but realised straight away that there was little point, as it would reach Harriet no sooner than he would himself. The afternoon was too far advanced for him to leave that day but he went in search of Cornelius, whom he found preparing to go shooting.

"With your permission, sir, I will join you. I am unfortunately called away and would enjoy the relaxation, before I leave, of attempting to bag a rabbit or two."

Little conversation passed between the two, but these days their silences were companionable.

"I have secured Winthrop's house, sir. I must thank you for the recommendation," Brew said as they walked through a gate into a large field.

"Good. It will suit you."

Later he disclosed to his father the reason for his early departure. "I don't know what I may be able to do to assist, but you will understand that I would wish to be there to give Harriet all the support I can."

"Of course. You need not worry about things here. Pullman has all in hand. I am certain you will be able to help Miss Lambert but, even if that is not the case, your presence must be a comfort to her."

When they sat down to dine that evening, Brew asked, "Would you wish to accompany me to London, sir, where I shall go first if that is your desire? It will be some weeks still before Mama and Becca return home."

"I think not. I am too old for all this gadding about." The squire put his elbows on the table, steepled his fingers and, looking directly at his son, continued gravely, "I have written an apology to your mother. I hope that when I see her again, we may begin to rebuild some of the bridges which I have been instrumental in breaking down. I have much time to make up for, and it isn't something I would wish to do in the gaze of London society."

Brew returned no answer. He was in no small way surprised that his father had taken him into his confidence in such a way, but it was witness to the vastly improved relations they were enjoying. He raised his glass, a salute which was returned with a warm smile the like of which he hadn't seen since he was a boy.

By the time Brew reached Merivale, Harriet had been there for three days and her habit of command had created a quite different atmosphere from the despair that had greeted her upon her arrival. Mary had at the recommendation of the doctor been moved back home to the care of her mother. It was a responsibility Harriet would have shouldered, but she admitted to Mrs Sweet that with everything they had to do, Mary would doubtless be better off where she was.

Edward Butterfield was her almost constant companion as they inspected the house together, deciding what could be salvaged and what must be abandoned. In the end, it was agreed that the house itself should be restored to its former state, but this would take some months. The most urgent consideration was that of the kitchen, for they had to eat. A temporary replacement was to be installed in the east wing, and work on this was to begin immediately. Brew walked in as this was being discussed, and Mr Butterfield tactfully withdrew as the couple embraced. Uncharacteristically, Harriet burst into tears on her lover's shoulder. He spent some moments comforting her before remarking that had he known she would be weeping on him, he would have brought a spare coat. This made her laugh, and he gently dabbed her cheeks.

"Have I ever told you what expressive eyes you have, my darling?"

"You haven't, and I hope they are at the moment telling you how happy I am to see you."

"I sincerely hope you will not weep every time we meet, for it will give people a bad opinion of me, I am sure."

She gurgled in response.

Brew put a finger under her chin and raised it so that he might kiss her gently on the lips before remarking, "That's better. Now, sit down, if you will, and tell me all that has occurred."

Harriet explained how much damage had been done and the plans she and the steward had put in place. For the next three days, they inspected the house, toured the estate and went riding. She alternated between Rhapsody and Brandy, and he rode Apollo.

"He suits you well, Brew. I know my father would have been pleased that his favourite has found a new home. You will take him, won't you?"

"Might your mother not have something to say to that?"

Harriet laughed. "Not she. You will have observed that she does not ride in London? Well, rarely does she do so in the country, though she does keep a mount here for those occasions. She uses carriages only as a convenience, a necessity to make her life more comfortable. With respect to horses, I am my father's daughter. No, she will be happy Apollo has a new owner, of course, but the affinity between you will have little meaning for her."

"Then I shall accept him gladly as your wedding gift to me. But what of you? Can you choose between Rhapsody and Brandy?"

"I neither can, nor do I need to. You have seen these past few days how much both mean to me. Why would I part with either?"

"I can think of no reason at all, my love," he said, laughing and urging his mount into a gallop. Quick to react, it was but moments before Harriet was matching him stride for stride and for a while the future was left to take care of itself.

They were inspecting the damage in the west wing one morning and discussing the schedule when Brew judged it time to broach something that had been worrying him.

"Have you discussed this with your mother, dearest?" He was, he realised, treading on ground as boggy as the marshes that lay a short distance from where they sat. "It may be that she will not wish to remain in such a large house with your sister already married and you shortly to be so."

Harriet looked at him as if she didn't understand what he was saying and then raised a hand to her cheek. "I hadn't thought! I cannot leave her alone! First my father, then Amabel, and now me. No, it is too much for her to bear. Oh, Brew, what are we to do? I cannot marry you under such circumstances."

He was as pale as she and dropped the hand he was holding. "Harriet, what are you saying?"

She looked at him, no vestige of colour in her cheeks.

Shocked as he was at her last remark, he knew it was incumbent upon him to rescue the situation from the potential disaster that loomed before them. He said, as gently as he could, "I think, from what I have seen of your mother, that she would not wish you to sacrifice your happiness, or indeed mine," he added with a wry smile, trying for a touch of lightness, "for a home which I believe is not as close to her heart as it is to yours. What worries me more is that you will not be happy away from Merivale. Could you not bear to live with me elsewhere?"

He watched as a number of emotions flickered across her face. Fear. Sadness. Apprehension. And, finally, despair.

"You are right, of course. Merivale means far more to me than it does to Mama. I had not before considered what a wrench it would be for me to leave. The fire and its repercussions have only accentuated to me my love for the place. But my home and my heart are where you are, Brew."

He took her hands once more, breathing a quiet sigh of relief, but it was short-lived.

"No, let me finish. First allow me to say how sorry I am to have given pause for even a moment. I would not for the world have you believe I could permit such a thing as a house to come between us. I cannot, however, proceed as we had planned. While I would live with you in a cottage, my mother's situation must first be resolved. I cannot even consider marriage until that is done. I must return to London to discuss her prospects as well as our own. Will you come with me?"

"To the ends of the earth."

No more was said, but the sparkle which had infected them both had gone as they now faced a very uncertain future.

Louisa was not at home when they arrived in London the following afternoon. The usually calm Harriet spoke with agitation.

"The biggest problem is that I cannot come up with a plan which I truly believe will make her happy and secure her future."

"But as yet you have been unable to ask her," Brew pointed out. "It may be that, unlike us, she had foreseen this predicament and has something of her own in mind. As she was not expecting us, it is hardly surprising she isn't at home on such a fine afternoon. I shall leave you now and return to Grosvenor Square. With your leave, I shall call again this evening, by which time I hope you and Louisa will have had ample opportunity to discuss and resolve the dilemma."

"I wish I had your confidence."

"Nonsense, Harriet. I have every faith in you. And in your mother." With which comment he left, hoping sincerely that his trust was not misplaced. After all, his future happiness depended on it.

An hour later, Louisa returned to Hay Hill. "What a lovely surprise, Harriet! I hadn't looked for you today and was sure you would be fixed at Merivale for some time to come."

"Brew joined me a few days ago and we decided to return to London, as there is something I need to discuss with you."

"That sounds serious. Give me a moment to remove my hat, for I came straight away to the morning room when the footman told me you were here."

She left the room and Harriet paced up and down, as ever a sign of her agitation, wondering how to broach the subject. She wasn't left waiting many moments. Her mother returned and sat with her hands folded demurely in her lap.

"You have already written to explain to me how things stand at Merivale, so tell me immediately what else is troubling you. Is there something amiss between you and your fiancé?"

"I am having misgivings, Mama."

"About Brew? Oh, surely not. You are so right for each other."

"It's more complicated than that." Harriet was so torn she couldn't prevent a sob from escaping her lips.

"Oh, my darling, tell me what's wrong," Louisa said, moving to sit beside her daughter and placing a comforting arm about her shoulders.

Instead of answering directly, Harriet posed a question of her own. "Tell me, Mama, what are your feelings for Merivale?"

Louisa looked baffled. "I don't understand your question."

"Papa took you there as his bride many years ago, but since his death, or even before then, you have shown little interest in the estate. But what of the house itself? Are you happy there?"

Louisa looked at her daughter, still unsure as to where this was leading. "I would have been happy with Percival wherever we had lived. As for Merivale, I love the house and Papa was so proud of it. Situated as it is, though, I have always felt somewhat isolated there. The landscape is bleak. Yes, I know you love it, but it can be a lonely place," she said as Harriet fidgeted for a moment. "There are few close neighbours, and you must know how much I enjoy the society of others. Is it this that's been worrying you?"

"I cannot allow you to live at Merivale on your own. I have told Brew that our marriage will not go ahead under such circumstances." Harriet was sitting bolt upright, twisting a fold in her dress between restless fingers.

"And you would sacrifice your happiness in such a way for me? Foolish girl, have you not already suffered enough loss in your life? I must tell you, then, what has occurred this afternoon. I have spent the time with your Aunt Matilda, something I've have been doing far more frequently of late. It's quite strange," she said with a mischievous smile. "We haven't always got along as well as we might in the past, but I have discovered recently that we have much in common and enjoy each other's company far more than either of us would have believed possible. We have today decided between us that, during the season, I shall remain in Hay Hill and she will reside in St James's Square. For the rest of the year, we will live together at Sawcroft House. I am in fact to return to my childhood home."

"Oh no, Mama, I could not have you make such a sacrifice!"

"You mistake the matter, my darling. Matilda and I will have separate apartments but shall, when we wish, come together. It will suit us both admirably. There is no sacrifice. It has in fact given me a new purpose, one which has been lacking since your father died. Marry your major, Harriet, and be happy. I am as certain as I can be that I shall be so."

"But what of Merivale?"

"Until today I could not have asked you to cease renovations, for I had no plan in place for myself, and indeed I believe it is right to undertake them. We will find a way to retain the house if you cannot bear to part with it. Not for me and not for Amabel, who is I know excited about moving to Lincolnshire. My advice would be to sell, but it is a decision you and Brew must reach together. As for the rest, my future is now assured. So tell me, what have you done with your young man?"

Harriet, who had of late become more able to show her feelings, shed tears, only this time they were happy tears. She explained that Brew would be paying them a visit that evening and that she could hardly wait to tell him that her fears had been laid to rest. They would at last be able to set a date for the wedding.

CHAPTER TWENTY-THREE

While he waited to return to Hay Hill, Brew's pent-up emotions found relief in a brisk walk to his club. Though he hadn't discarded his stick, his gait was so much improved as to render it almost redundant. Once there he spent a while playing cards although, on account of his natural aptitude, it didn't hold his attention as he might have wished.

Finally it was time to meet his fate. It was with trepidation that he rapped on the Lamberts' door and waited. The footman was by now well acquainted with the major and showed him immediately to the drawing room. Taking a deep breath, he paused in the doorway before entering, his eyes seeking Harriet's. Just a glance was enough, for the look she cast him brought sunshine back into his heart. It enabled him to greet Louisa with the charm that was habitual to him before moving to his fiancée and kissing her fingertips. His grin, to the fore once more, brought a similar response from the ladies.

"I see that I find you both well and in good spirits, and I will not hesitate to inform you that my mind is much relieved," he said. "I have spent a very uncomfortable few hours, I can tell you. May I know what you have concocted between you in so short a time as to be able to ensure my future happiness?"

It took only a few minutes to apprise Brew of the proposed arrangement. It was one of which he heartily approved, having affection both for his future mother-in-law and for Lady Sawcroft. Though he professed to be in awe of Harriet's aunt, she vastly appealed to him, for she lacked neither humour nor backbone.

"Then I take it we may now put in place some firm arrangements for our wedding? In light of what you have told me, and if I may be permitted to do so, I would consider it an honour to purchase Merivale as a gift for my bride."

Harriet's eyes were round with astonishment. "But, Brew, why would you want two homes? Surely our plan was to live in Lincolnshire."

He looked at her with so much affection that she felt herself melt. His answer too was everything she could have wished. "It is simple. During my two brief visits, I have developed a fondness for the place. The terrain is such that I imagine might be found in only a few places. Riding on the Kent marshes is like nothing I have ever experienced and is not something I would relinquish gladly. Did you think my motive was only to please you? You are merely my excuse."

"What a rogue you are, sir. But if that is your wish and if my mother agrees, then I accept gladly."

"Then tell me, if you will, what are your wishes. Shall we be wed in St George's as we had anticipated?"

"I have been thinking, Brew. In only a very few weeks, your mother and sister will return to Austerly. Amabel and Gil too will be in Lincolnshire. It would be unkind to drag your father to London when you know of his reluctance to travel. Sarah and Matthew also will be going home. There remain only you and I, Mama and Lady Sawcroft, and I know my aunt would happily welcome an invitation, for a more inquisitive person I have never yet met."

"And not only Matilda," Louisa laughed. "I am as curious as the next person."

Brew's face clouded over and both were dismayed in case they had offended him. He made haste to reassure them. "The work at Austerly is not yet complete. I would wish you to see it when all is done, for it is a beautiful house but still in need of much care and attention." He paused and walked to the window, his fingers absentmindedly playing with the drapes. "On the other hand," he continued, turning back to face them, "reparations are underway, and we still have some time at our disposal. If the bedchambers are not yet up to scratch, those at Winthrop most certainly are. We could house our visitors there. What say you, then? Shall we make a push for Austerly?"

"Only if you wish it, dearest."

"Wish it? I would count it an honour."

Louisa rose and said, "Then I shall leave the two of you to discuss the finer details while I go and speak to Cook. You will stay to dine, Major?"

"Thank you, that would be most welcome."

After she had gone, Harriet spent a few minutes demonstrating her appreciation before Brew put her away from him. "There is a downside to all of this, you know. It will necessitate us being parted yet again, for there will be much to do before the place is fit to entertain visitors. Though a letter to my steward would set everything in train, I must admit I would prefer to be there myself to oversee things, admirable though Pullman is."

"I understand perfectly, and I'm sure I would be the same myself. There is one thing I would ask of you, Brew." Harriet looked hesitant for a moment. "It is something I can arrange myself, but I would be so very grateful, when the horses are moved from Merivale to Austerly, if Ben and Arthur might go with them. They are the head groom and under groom, you understand. Naturally Mrs Sweet would remain, and the rest of the staff too, and Edward Butterfield will maintain all when we are not there, but Ben has been with me since I was a child and Arthur too is devoted to my interests. I am certain it is to me and not the house that they owe their allegiance and, well, it was Ben who put me on my first pony."

Harriet was lifted off her feet and swung around before being placed tenderly back on the floor.

"You are, my darling, without equal. Of course they must come, and any other of your people you would choose to have with you. I have as yet engaged no staff for Winthrop, so that is one task you have saved me from. It isn't as large as Austerly, nor yet Merivale, but I truly believe you will love it. I give you leave here and now to decorate the place from top to bottom if it does not meet with your approval. I made certain also before hiring it that the stables were adequate, for I know that is one thing upon which there can be no compromise."

The couple were delighted and spent the next two days laying down plans. When the time arrived for Brew to ride north, it came as a shock to them both.

Harriet put on a brave face, saying, "You must go now and make all ready. Do not worry about me, for I shall be so busy I will barely have time to notice you are not here."

"I beg your pardon?"

She threw him a look so arch as to make him grin, but it was only to cover her sadness at his leaving. "Just think, sir. I have bride clothes to purchase, and of course I shall kit out myself and my mother in only the finest that may be found. Then there will be letters to write to Merivale, invitations to honour and a hundred other things to do. In fact, I cannot imagine why I have not sent you away sooner."

Brew crushed her in his arms and gave her to understand that there had been very good reasons. He left an emptiness behind him which she attempted to fill in a whirlwind of activity, for the purchase of a trousseau was no small matter to any young woman.

In the midst of all this turmoil, Mr and Mrs Carstairs returned to London. Gil, having escorted his wife to his mother-in-law's home and paid his respects to her and to Harriet, departed for an urgent visit to his tailor.

"He was so taken with the latest fashion in Paris that nothing would do but to have it copied straight away," Amabel said with obvious amusement and no little affection. "How do your own plans go, Harriet?"

Harriet looked at Louisa, her consternation quite evident.

"What is it? What has happened?"

"We didn't want to distress you while you were away, but there has been a serious fire at Merivale. Arthur came to fetch me but there was little I could do, or anyone else for that matter. Fortunately it had been extinguished by the time I got there."

The younger sister clutched her throat. "Is the house gone, then?"

"Thank heaven, no, but the west wing is damaged beyond repair and must be completely rebuilt. Edward Butterfield has been of the utmost support to me and all is now in hand, but it will take some months and I hate not being there to supervise."

"And then what, Harriet? Are you and Brew not to take up residence in Lincolnshire?" She turned to Louisa. "Mama?"

"You will see now why we did not write to you, dearest. The details were far too complicated to put in a letter, but you may be at ease. All is settled very satisfactorily." She went on to explain the plans for her own future and for Merivale too.

"How very kind of Brew, and how good that the house will not be leaving the family. But you, Mama! You are to live for some of the year with Aunt Matilda!"

She was obviously incredulous and it took some time to convince her that it was indeed her mother's wish to do so.

"And now it's your turn, Amabel. Mama and I are keen for you to tell us all about Paris."

Amabel clasped her hands together with an enthusiasm she didn't attempt to hide. "It is beyond anything, Harriet. The Louvre. Notre Dame. The River Seine. Well, nothing compares with the Thames, of course, not in my opinion, but as a setting for the cathedral it is truly beautiful. You must insist you go there when you are married. Gil tells me Brew knows it far better than he, for he lived there for three years after the war, didn't he? Now, let us discuss more important matters, like the plans for your wedding. You may imagine how anxious I am to go to my new home, but naturally we will remain in London until then."

"Then let me relieve your mind, my darling sister. Brew is even now at Austerly, putting all in train for us to be married there. It makes far more sense for us to do so, particularly as it is no longer easy for his father to travel. Though I shall bear your advice very much in mind, we will not be leaving England for a while yet. What with the renovations there, a new home at Winthrop, and then the work at Merivale, well, we shall be employed for some time to come."

Amabel joined eagerly in a number of shopping expeditions before departing the capital. While she tearfully embraced her mother and sister, nothing could hide her excitement at the prospect of her and Gil truly beginning their new life together.

"Well, Mama, you may dry your own tears, for it will not be many days now before Brew returns to escort us to Austerly. Is my aunt ready to go, do you know? Are you certain you wish to travel in her carriage rather than with me?"

"I am indeed. We will follow you a day later, for we must both, Aunt Matilda and I, ensure all is in order for shutting down the houses for the summer. I would far rather see you safely on your way before I make my final tour."

By the time Brew returned to London, it seemed unlikely that the number of bandboxes and trunks stored ready for transport north would all fit in one carriage. Harriet enjoyed shopping as much as the next young woman, but some of the things strapped up and waiting had come from Merivale. She had taken the opportunity to go and collect anything she didn't feel she could part with, or do without for any length of time. It seemed like a good moment, for it might be many months before she and Brew would travel into Kent. She grasped his hand and dragged him to the room, excited for him to see. When he did, he near exploded with laughter at the vast number of things waiting to be moved. It was infectious, and soon the two of them were clutching their sides.

"It's all very well, but some of these belonged to my father," Harriet explained. "I was sure you would understand."

Brew smiled affectionately. "I do, of course. I suppose I should be grateful you didn't bring Apollo. You didn't, did you?" he asked, suddenly alarmed that the horse might even now be stabled nearby.

"No, because you said you would travel with me by carriage. Had I thought there was any possibility we might ride together, I could well have done so."

"Then I must be grateful for that, at least. It is my intention to visit my mother and sister tomorrow. I would deem it a favour if you would come with me. Then perhaps we may leave the following day, for I am anxious now to take you home. My family are not planning to return until the end of the week."

"I should be delighted. But I cannot stay at Austerly with you before we are married!"

"Of course not. I have taken the liberty of engaging staff at Winthrop, and it was my intention that you should go there with your maid. Pru, my old nurse, has agreed to stay with you until such time as other arrangements can be made, or until after the wedding. And of course your mother and Lady Sawcroft will be joining us within twenty-four hours."

"It seems you have thought of everything."

"To be honest, I think Pru can't wait to meet you and no doubt will confide in you some of my worst misdemeanours as a child."

"In that case, I must tell you it is a provision with which I am delighted to concur."

They left Elizabeth wiping her eyes with her handkerchief on the day of their departure. Having been reunited with her son after so long, her inclination was to keep him by her side, but she smiled through her tears.

"We will join you, Becca and I, sometime next week. You may imagine my curiosity in seeing what changes you have made to my home. Your father writes that he is well pleased, though I doubt he would admit as much to you."

Brew laughed. "Assuredly he would not. His pride would never allow it, but I left him in good spirits and I am optimistic about our future dealings."

"I can only judge from his letters, of course, but it is apparent to me he is a changed man, and for that I have you to thank."

"We are both changed, Mama," he said, serious for a moment. "And now I fear we must leave," he added, taking Harriet's hand in his. She withdrew it immediately, but only so she might embrace Elizabeth and Rebecca. There had been no chance of private conversation, and she was concerned for Becca. It would take her some time to recover from her amorous adventure, but she looked well enough. Harriet could only hope time would work its magic.

The couple walked from Duke Street to Hay Hill, where Brew had arranged for their carriage to be waiting. They took only the things they would need for their journey, the rest being loaded into a second vehicle which was piled high with Harriet's belongings and would go straight to Winthrop. Harriet's maid travelled with them, and thus conversation was restricted to the ordinary. By the time they reached Austerly the following day, the couple were feeling the frustration of having to utter nothing but mundanities when they had so much they wished to discuss.

Proud but nervous, Brew handed his fiancée down from the carriage. She looked up at his childhood home, an imposing edifice which she liked upon sight. The door was flung wide by Kettersham and she entered the hall to find Cornelius Ware, who was standing before the oak staircase waiting to greet them.

"My dear, may I be the first to welcome you to my home and to say what a pleasure it is to see you here." Was this the seemingly cold man Harriet had met in London? "Come on, boy, bring her in. Bring her in."

Harriet moved forward and the old man took her hand.

"You know of our circumstances, so I shall not prevaricate. It is my sincere hope that you will be happy here, though not for a while yet, I hope," he added, chuckling. "In the meantime, Brew has hired a very pretty house which is no great distance away, and you must feel able to come here any time you wish. I know my wife will be glad of it."

Harriet tried to hide her surprise and was adequately successful, as his humour had brought her own to the surface. She could for the first time see in him the charm that was so abundant in his son. "You must believe me, sir, when I say that I hope it will be many years before I take up residence at Austerly. In the meantime, I can only pray you will not grow tired of me visiting, for I can see already that it is a beautiful home. I look forward to seeing more of it."

"And so you shall, my dear, but first," he said, turning to the butler, "Kettersham, summon a footman, if you would, to take Miss Lambert to the blue room where she may refresh herself." He turned back to Harriet. "Please join me and my son in the drawing room when you are ready. There is no hurry; we will await dinner at your convenience."

Pru was waiting for her in the room to which her luggage had already been taken. Her maid was nowhere to be seen, and the old nurse explained that she had taken the liberty of dismissing her for the moment. Harriet put her hand out immediately, a warm smile lighting up her features.

"I have heard so much about you from the major. He speaks of you with such affection, and I must tell you he is terrified of the things you might tell me about his childhood. Such a naughty boy, he has given me to understand."

She sat down, in no hurry yet to change her clothes as she was eager for any information Pru might give her about Brew. They had a delightful cose and some considerable time had passed before they realised that in spite of the squire's assurances, it was time to dress for dinner.

"I understand you are to come with me to Winthrop. Are we to go this evening?" Harriet asked, looking out of the window. There was no moon that night, and she thought the journey might be hazardous in the dark.

"If you are happy to do so, miss, the squire did ask as how you might stay here tonight with your maid sleeping in the antechamber next door and me just down the corridor to make all right and tight, as it were."

This time Harriet laughed aloud. "I would back you against any number of men to protect me, Miss… I don't know what to call you."

"Pru. Or Nurse. Whichever you're comfortable with."

"Do you have a preference?"

The old woman smiled. "It's been a long time since anyone called me Nurse."

"Then Nurse it shall be. I am happy to assign myself to your care, though I do think that for form's sake we should go to Winthrop tomorrow."

"So be it. The master will be pleased, I know."

With a good relationship well on the way to being established, Harriet went downstairs to join the men for dinner.

CHAPTER TWENTY-FOUR

Had Harriet not herself had the doubtful pleasure of experiencing the squire's bad humour while in London, she might have been forgiven for disbelieving all that had been said about him. The man with whom she sat down to dine bore no resemblance to the grumpy, not to say rude, gentleman she had met on previous occasions. Keeping her reflections to herself, she was able to enjoy this seeming change in personality. Not only from politeness, but out of interest too, she said, "Your son has told me little about Austerly. From what I have seen, it is a home of which you are justly proud."

"No doubt he has also informed you that he is funding long-required renovations." His smile took any sting out of his words, but Harriet was surprised to find Cornelius so open about the situation. It must have shown on her face, because he said, "No point in hiding the truth. My pride was at first greatly wounded, but where's the use in indulging in a fit of the dismals when there's a need for change? Perhaps tomorrow, prior to your departure for Winthrop, you might like Brew to give you a tour of the place. I would go with you, but all this climbing up and down stairs does little for my constitution. I hope you will join me for a light luncheon, though, before you leave. And may I say, for perhaps I did not make it clear sooner, how happy I am to welcome you to the family. Elizabeth speaks very highly of you, and I know you have been a good friend to Rebecca."

For one dreadful moment Harriet suspected he knew about his daughter's elopement, but she realised soon enough that he spoke only of her aid in easing Becca into society.

"I had hoped she might have found herself a husband while in London," Cornelius went on. "It may be that she will have the opportunity to go again. In the meantime, she has at least gained some valuable experience."

"It is certain that your son and I will spend some time in town next year. I could not forego the opportunity of seeing my own mother, who I know plans to spend the season there. Perhaps, if Elizabeth wishes to remain at Austerly, Becca might come to us. It would give me great pleasure, for I have enjoyed her company immensely."

"You see, Father, already my bride is organising my life for me!" Brew put in. "She is a managing female — did I mention that to you? No doubt I shall soon become henpecked and quail every time she walks into the room."

A look of deep affection passed between the couple as Brew placed his hand upon Harriet's where it rested on the table.

"I suspect yours will be a lively marriage, for I say without judgement that neither of you are modest nor retiring," Cornelius laughed. "And, speaking of retiring, my bed is calling to me. I shall look forward to seeing you both at breakfast."

He did indeed look tired as he rose and left the room, and Harriet was reminded that he was an elderly man and not in good health. However, he had given back as good as he got during dinner, and she was as sure as she could be that he had enjoyed their lively exchanges. Brew confirmed this to be so when he said, "My father is a changed man, Harriet. As you are aware, life has not been easy for him. It is my earnest wish that his latter years may be spent in peace."

She agreed but laughed and said, "Peace? There is no doubt in my mind that he enjoys a spirited discussion and that such interactions will do far more for his health than sitting in a bath chair with a blanket over his knees."

"You are a fount of wisdom, my darling. I shall in future look to you to keep the old man suitably entertained. And now I think perhaps we too should retire, for it has been a long day. In the morning, if you are happy for it to be so, I shall do as my father suggested. Then we must hope that the carriage with our belongings will have preceded us to Winthrop, where I shall have the pleasure of escorting you about that property too."

The next day, Harriet and Brew spent a while touring Austerly and he was able to see what progress had been made during his short absence.

"I am pleased with the way things are coming along but, as you can observe, there is much to be done."

"Yes, and while a good deal of it is superficial, I can see there are slight damages to the structure here and there. On the whole, though, the task seems not to be as daunting as I had imagined."

"That's true. Most of the real work required is on the estate rather than the house itself, and that will not affect our visitors when we come to be married. It is fortunate that we can accommodate our wedding guests at Winthrop, for I do not hesitate to tell you that many of the bedchambers here are in a sorry state. As for the rest, to be honest I am astonished at the speed with which the work is being done. Come, allow me to show you the dining room. Not the one we used yesterday, but the formal room which has already been completed."

Brew led Harriet into a large and very imposing room, and for the first time she could see the potential glory of this beautiful old house. She gasped with pleasure and he, delighted with her reaction, offered to show her where they would be receiving their family and friends upon their return from the church where the ceremony was to take place. Its tall arched windows faced onto the garden, sadly still in a state of neglect, but the room itself was magnificent, the panelled walls on one side decorated with softly patterned cream paper. Furniture, which he told her had only arrived a week earlier, was comprised of two console tables that filled the spaces between the three panels, and a wide marble-topped chest was set against the opposite wall. Other occasional tables were dotted about the place together with various settees and mahogany-armed chairs upholstered in striking stripes of dark and light gold.

"It's quite dazzling, Brew," said Harriet.

"You don't like it?" he asked quickly.

"I think it the perfect place for entertaining and I wouldn't change a thing. The chandeliers are particularly tasteful, not too ornate but with something about them that is pleasing to the eye. But where do you sit when it is just family?"

"I believe it is my father's custom to sit in his library. My mother has her own withdrawing room, but I will not take you there today. That will be for her to show you, and I have as yet undertaken no alterations. I would not do so without her consent. There is another small drawing room and it may be that you would like to make some suggestions, as I haven't been able to decide what will best suit. It is a far more intimate space than the formal room from which we have just come."

Harriet was flattered that he should ask her opinion. The morning flew by, and after a hurried luncheon they left for Winthrop, anxious to be there before the arrival of Louisa and Aunt Matilda.

Harriet ran from room to room with the excitement of a child. This, after all, was to be her new home, and Brew observed a youthful enthusiasm he had never before seen in her. He was enchanted, and it was a very happy couple who welcomed Mrs Lambert and Lady Sawcroft only two hours after their own arrival.

"Mama, you must come and see the room we have allocated for you," Harriet said, tugging her mother's hand. "You too, Aunt Matilda. We have ourselves only been here a short while and all is still new to me."

Lady Sawcroft remarked that her niece had not after all outgrown all her hoydenish ways, but there was an approving smile in her eyes. It had been decided that with the advent of Harriet's mother and aunt, there was no need for Pru to act as chaperone and she had thus remained at Austerly. When Brew made to return there after a light supper, he was amused to note that his fiancée barely gave him a second glance, so deep in conversation was she with her family.

"I shall return tomorrow afternoon and hope you will have a few moments to spare for me," he jested.

Harriet threw such a mischievous glance at him that it was fortunate indeed that she was attended, for he would have found it hard to tear himself away.

Things were no different the next day, for her luggage, having been delayed by some twenty-four hours, arrived at much the same time as Brew did and naturally she had first to attend to that.

"I should perhaps have made an appointment he see you," he said, somewhat ironically.

Harriet only laughed and said, "Yes, but you know my penchant for organising. I cannot bear to see everything lying around and, while it is my maid who will naturally store things away, I should like to have some hand in the process."

"Then with your permission I shall escort your mother and Lady Sawcroft around the gardens."

"Yes, do," she replied before flitting upstairs to see to the disposal of her wardrobe.

The next day heralded the arrival of Rhapsody and Brandy, together with Apollo. While there was no question of taking them out after their long journey, Harriet and Brew spent a long while in the stables, seeing them settled, whispering in their ears and taking a brush to their manes and flanks. It was a happy day and the prelude to a period of pleasure they would remember all their lives.

Harriet visited Austerly only once before the wedding, riding over with Brew, who had come to escort her back. It was two days after Elizabeth and Rebecca returned home, and even in that short time she was able to observe a softening in the squire and his lady. She managed only a few words in private with Becca but was immediately reassured.

"I can never thank you enough for saving me from that dreadful man. I am quite over him, you know," Becca said. "While I do not despair of finding my prince, I am at present content."

"Then we shall say no more on the subject, and next season I hope you will join me and your brother when we return to London."

Two days later, Major Benedict Richmond Edward Ware was joined in holy matrimony to Miss Harriet Georgiana Lambert. The small church was filled to capacity as neighbours and local dignitaries joined the families for the ceremony. The newly refurbished room at Austerly, while not crowded, was nevertheless sufficiently occupied not to seem overly large for the occasion, the squire having taken great pleasure in inviting one and all. After doing their duties as hosts, Brew and Harriet slipped away into the garden and he led her along the back of the house until they stood outside his mother's drawing room. It was thus that for the first time Harriet saw the wishing well, and she quickly glanced up at her husband, anxious and curious at the same time.

"I wanted to show you," he said, and she was happy to see that he was smiling. "It is the only thing I have so far not shared with you. Like my mother, I have found it now brings me solace rather than pain."

It had indeed been rendered safe and was a beautiful structure such that one might see at any number of properties. But this one held a significance that others did not.

"It gives me great comfort to know that, while Nancy is no longer with you, she will never be forgotten," said Harriet.

She bent down to see what was obviously a newly inscribed stone on the front of the well. It simply read:

Nancy
Forever in our hearts

"For once in my life, Brew, I don't have the words," Harriet murmured.

Brew raised her with his hands and drew her towards him. His thumbs brushed away her tears. "No words are needed. I brought you here not just to share my past but also to make a wish for the future. It is, after all, still a wishing well. You have given me a happiness I never thought to have, Harriet, and my hope is that I can bring such joy into your life as you have to mine. It is my earnest desire that in years to come, whenever we visit the well, it will be to give thanks for a life well lived."

"So too is it my wish, Brew. We have both of us had our measure of sorrow. From this day, whatever life brings, we will share it together."

A NOTE TO THE READER

Dear Reader

I hope you have enjoyed reading *The Wishing Well* as much as I enjoyed writing it. If you would consider leaving a review on **Amazon** or **Goodreads**, it would be much appreciated, though I would be just as happy if you'd like to join me on my **Facebook author page** for a chat. You can also visit me on **Twitter**, **Instagram** and my **website**.

Natalie

nataliekleinman.com

SAPERE BOOKS

Sapere Books is an exciting new publisher of brilliant fiction and popular history.

To find out more about our latest releases and our monthly bargain books visit our website: **saperebooks.com**

Printed in Great Britain
by Amazon